THE GUNS OF FORT GRIFFIN

Center Point
Large Print

Also by James J. Griffin and available from Center Point Large Print:

The Ranger
The Zombies of Zapata
Bullet for a Ranger
Ride for Justice, Ride for Revenge
Trouble Times Two
Desperate Ride
Change of Venue
Death Comes to Lajitas
Catch a Falling Star
Tall Trouble in Terlingua
Rough Riders of the Ragged Rimrock
Trouble Percolates in Coffee City
Deadly Trail

U. S. Marshal Vic Verdugo

THE GUNS OF FORT GRIFFIN

A WESTERN ADVENTURE

James J. Griffin

CENTER POINT LARGE PRINT
THORNDIKE, MAINE

This Center Point Large Print edition
is published in the year 2026 by arrangement with
the author.

The text of this Large Print edition is unabridged.
In other aspects, this book may vary
from the original edition.
Printed in the United States of America
on permanent paper sourced using
environmentally responsible foresting methods.
Set in 16-point Times New Roman type.

ISBN: 979-8-89164-782-4

The Library of Congress has cataloged this record
under Library of Congress Control Number: 2025947297

THE GUNS OF FORT GRIFFIN

1

"Marshal, either come out of there, or we'll burn you out."

"And if I do, you'll gun me down the minute I show myself. Do you think I'm a damn fool, Bohannon? I'll take my chances none of you will be able to get close enough to throw a torch into this shack. Whoever tries will take a bullet first."

Momentary silence ensued. Deputy United States Marshal Victor Verdugo cursed himself.

"Actually, you *are* a damn fool, Verdugo, letting yourself get cornered like this. Even a rookie wouldn't have made such a bad mistake."

Vic was on the trail of David Bohannon and his outlaw brothers, Bob and Bill. The trio was wanted for horse thieving and murder, crimes they'd committed throughout central Texas. He had followed them to the small settlement of Hornsby Bend, which was located on a sharp curve of the Colorado River, about a dozen miles east of Austin. Somehow he'd allowed the brothers to get behind him. It was pure luck he was able to outrace them to the shack where he was now holed up.

Topper, his Medicine Hat paint, had crowded into the shack with his rider, where he was relatively safe from gunfire. He rolled his eyes at

Vic and snorted, seeming to agree with him.

"I can cuss myself out quite well without your help, hoss!"

Several more bullets crashed into the shack, two penetrating its flimsy walls.

"Marshal, that was your last warn . . . *unhhh*."

Dave Bohannon's last words were cut off when Vic took careful aim and put a bullet right through his open mouth, the .44 caliber slug taking out most of the gang leader's teeth, tearing through his tongue, and burying itself in the back of his brain. He was dead before he hit the dirt.

"You just killed Dave," Bob Bohannon shouted. "You'll die for that, Verdugo."

"I intended to do just that," Vic answered. "You and your brother throw out your guns and come out with your hands in the air, or you'll get the same."

Bill Bohannon leaned from behind the cottonwood tree where he'd taken cover. Vic took quick aim and shot him in the chest, then, when he stumbled out into plain view, put a second bullet into him. Two of three Bohannons now lay stretched out on the ground, dead.

"I give up!" Bob shouted. "Here's my gun. I'm coming out."

He tossed a six-gun into the grass, then with his hands in the air stood up from behind the log he'd used for cover.

Vic came outside, his gun at the ready. As soon

as he did, the last Bohannon brother dug for the belly gun he had hidden under his shirt. Vic shot him through the gut. Bob clamped his hands to his middle, folded in half, fell face down and then rolled onto his back.

His smoking six-gun still in his hand, Vic walked up to the badly wounded outlaw. He reached inside Bob's shirt, pulled out the short-barreled .38 caliber Remington hidden there, and tossed it aside.

"Damn you to Hell, Marshal. You done kilt both my brothers, and you've kilt me, too. You lived up to your name, all right."

Verdugo meant "Executioner" in Spanish.

"You ain't dead yet, Bohannon, unlike so many folks you and your brothers killed in cold blood. If I can get you to a doctor right quick, he might be able to pull you through. We're not all that far from Austin."

He took the bandanna from around Bob's neck, stuffed it inside his shirt.

"Keep holdin' that neckerchief tight over the hole in your belly. It'll slow the blood flow, so maybe you won't bleed out."

Vic gathered the Bohannons' guns and shoved them in his saddlebags, then got their horses. He loaded the two dead men, draping them belly down over their saddles and lashing them in place. He helped Bob onto his horse, tying his ankles to the stirrups.

“Let me know if you need to stop,” he told Bob, as he climbed into his own saddle. “I’ll move as fast as I can without jouncing you all over the place.”

2

As the state capital, Austin was more settled than many of the other cities in Texas. People weren't used to the sight of a United States Deputy Marshal leading two horses carrying dead bodies, and a third with a wounded man slumped over in the saddle, along Congress Avenue toward the State Capitol, no less in the middle of the day.

Vic stopped at Doctor William Middleton's office first. Middleton was the Travis County Coroner, so he would leave the bodies with him, along with Bob Bohannon, who was still clinging to life.

"I don't imagine he'll live through the night, but I'll try my best to save him, Marshal," Middleton said. "Not that it will make much difference, since I imagine if he does pull through the state will hang him anyway."

"Most likely," Vic agreed. "I'm going to head for the office, check in and make my report. Then I hope I'll get a couple of days to rest, but I doubt it."

"Would you like me to write a letter stating you're exhausted, and need some time off?"

"It's a tempting thought, but I'll pass for now. Perhaps another time."

"Whenever you need one," Middleton said.

"I'm obliged, Doc. *Adios*."

"*Adios*, Marshal."

Vic rode the short distance to the United States District Judge's Office, which was near the State Capitol Building. He allowed Topper to drink his fill from the horse trough out front, then tied his reins to an iron horsehead hitching post.

"I shouldn't be all that long, I hope," he told the gelding, with a pat to his nose. "Soon as I'm done we'll head for home. I'm as eager to put on the feedbag as you are."

Topper nickered, then began scratching the side of his head on the post.

Vic went inside the building, then down a long, wainscoted corridor to Judge Isaiah Canton's office. Canton was the chief federal justice for all of Texas, and the United States Marshals and Deputies for the state reported directly to him.

Canton was seated behind his heavy black walnut desk when Vic walked in, going through a case file. He looked up, was pleasantly surprised to see one of his best deputies back sooner than expected. Canton was in his early sixties, with gray hair and beard, piercing hazel eyes, and quite overweight from his sedentary lifestyle.

"Well hello, Vic. I didn't think you'd return for a few more days. Were you able to run down the Bohannon brothers?"

"I was, Judge. They put up a fight. Dave and

Bill are dead, Bob is at Doc Middleton's with one of my slugs in his gut. The doc says he probably won't live through the night."

"If he doesn't, that will save the expense of a trial and execution," Canton said. "Good work, Vic. Would you care for a cigar?"

"That does sound good."

Canton took two cigars from the rosewood humidor on his desk, handed one to Vic. Both men lit up, each taking a large puff on his cigar and sending bluish-gray smoke rings toward the ceiling.

"How soon will you have your report completed?" Canton asked.

"I can prepare it right now if you'd like. It should only take me an hour or so."

"There's no need to rush it. Get yourself some rest first. I almost hate to ask you this, but how soon will you be ready to ride out again?"

"As soon as you need me to."

"Excellent. I've got a tough assignment, one which I can trust only a few of my men with. You're the only one available at the moment. Why don't you take tomorrow to get a bit of rest and procure everything you and your horse will need for a long journey, then leave the day after?"

"I can manage that, Judge. Where are we headed?"

"You mean where are *you* headed, Deputy. This is a solo assignment."

"I was including Topper."

Canton laughed.

"Naturally. Your horse. What was I thinking?"

"I can't do my job without him," Vic pointed out.

"I suppose that is true. As far as where you're going, I'm sending you to Fort Griffin. Do you know anything about the place?"

"Just what I've heard, which is that it's a real hellhole."

"Hellhole is an understatement. I do believe Satan himself wouldn't dare to set foot into the place. He'd be chased out of town if he tried."

Canton took another pull on his cigar before continuing.

"The Army fort was there first. Most of the enlisted men are buffalo soldiers, the officers white. It didn't take long for a town to spring up once the fort was established. You know the kind of denizens who populate such a place."

"Let's see. Outlaws, con artists, thieves, gamblers, and whores come to mind first off."

"At Fort Griffin, those *are* the honest folks. Murderers and vicious *hombres* of all stripes plague the place. There's trouble between the blacks and whites. It's also a center for buffalo hunters, and all the problems they bring. Needless to say, you won't be welcomed with open arms."

"I'm usually not," Vic said, with a rueful grin.

"It gets even more complicated. The governor

wants the place cleaned up. The Army wants to take over control of the town themselves, so you won't be able to expect any help from them. They'll keep pushing to declare martial law."

"I'll try to avoid stepping on their toes."

"The Army might be the least of your problems. As you know, Reconstruction is coming to an end. President Grant recently signed the order readmitting Texas to the Union and ending Congressional Reconstruction. However, there are many pressing matters which will need to be settled before Texas can, in fact, govern herself again."

Canton stopped to catch his breath, then went on.

"The State Police are still the official law enforcement agency. You're well aware they are despised by most Texans, and people are fighting to have them disbanded. Most honest folks want the Texas Rangers restored."

"That would be one of the best things that could happen to bring outlawry to an end."

"Since you were a Ranger until the outfit was disbanded, I expected to hear that. However, you have to realize there are still many citizens who resent the Rangers and some of their actions, even to this day. There are many whites who want to keep the Negroes in their place, and would like nothing better than to see some form of slavery return. The Negroes are pressuring for equal rights with the whites. And just about everyone wants the Yankee carpetbaggers, and their scalawag cohorts, run out of Texas, along with the Federal troops. You'll not only have to rid Fort Griffin of the bad elements, but also be a diplomat. You'll need to walk a fine line between all the various factions. I'm counting on you to do just that, Vic. Even though diplomat is one name I've never heard attached to you."

"I'll do my best, Judge."

"That's all I ask. How soon do you believe it will take to reach the town?"

"It's about two hundred and thirty miles from here to Fort Griffin. If I ride steadily, without pushing too hard, it will take me about eight days. I can cover the distance in half that if you need me to."

"That won't be necessary. I'd rather you arrived at least somewhat rested, rather than worn out."

"I agree with you there. If there's nothing else, I'll check in with you before I leave. I'll need to drop off my report on the Bohannon case in any event."

"That's just fine, Vic. Have a good evening."

"You also, Judge."

3

Vic owned a small house on the outskirts of Austin. It was compact but well kept, its wooden clapboards painted white, the shutters a deep shade of blue, commonly called Federal Blue. The inside was divided into three tidy rooms, a living room with fireplace, bedroom, and kitchen. The rooms were sparsely furnished, a sofa, overstuffed chair, and two tables on which stood lamps in the living room, a single bed, side table with lamp, and bureau in the bedroom. Vic's Mexican heritage meant he was raised a Roman Catholic, so a crucifix hung on the wall above the bed. The kitchen held a square oak table with two ladder-back chairs, an oak breakfront, two wall cabinets, wood stove, and a wooden sink with a pump. The only décor in the house was some Navajo rugs on the living room floor, another at the foot of the bed. All in all, it was a fitting abode for a lifelong bachelor who spent much of his time away from home, roaming the Lone Star State, enforcing the law.

There was a two-stall barn and a small corral behind the house. Vic led Topper there. He got the gear off his horse, put out his hay and grain, and a bucket of water. He groomed the Medicine Hat while Topper worked on his supper.

"Enjoy yourself tonight, pard. It might be the last good rest either of us will have for quite some time."

After giving Topper a piece of leftover biscuit, Vic headed inside. He had bought some supplies after leaving Judge Canton, so he wouldn't have to pay for a restaurant meal. He got a fire going in the stove, put on ham and eggs to fry, and a pot of coffee to brew. He washed up at the sink while the food cooked, then once it was done settled down to his supper. After washing and drying the dishes, he drank a last cup of coffee and smoked one last cigarette, then undressed and got into bed. He picked up his rosary beads from the bedside table. Although he no longer got to church to attend Mass very often, he still prayed the Rosary every night. He, as did many Mexicans and Mexican Americans, had a special devotion to the Blessed Virgin Mary, particularly as *Nuestra Senora de Guadalupe.*

Two whole nights in my own bed, with my own roof over my head and my horse comfortable in his own barn. Damned if I can't understand why I don't just up and quit, stay home and become a county deputy or Austin police officer.

Vic drifted off to sleep with that thought in his head.

Vic spent the next day preparing for his trip. He stopped by the blacksmith shop to have new shoes put on Topper, all around. He got all the supplies he could fit in his saddlebags, including extra ammunition for his pistol and rifle, peppermint sticks for Topper's treats. He finished up the day by stopping at Lou's Tonsorial Parlor for a haircut, shave, and bath. It would be quite some time before he had that chance again. After his cleanup, he had supper at a nearby café, then headed for home.

"You get yourself plenty of rest tonight, pal," he told Topper, as he finished grooming him and turned him loose in the corral. "It's gonna be quite some time before you see your own barn again."

Topper nudged at him, knowing Vic had a candy in his vest pocket. He nickered impatiently.

Vic laughed.

"All right, ya big beggar. Here ya go."

Vic gave the paint his treat, then smacked him a fond slap on the neck.

"See you in the morning."

Vic headed inside, undressed and stretched out on his bed. He murmured a few evening prayers, the Rosary, then drifted off to sleep.

4

Vic started out just after sunrise. He harbored no illusions about covering the two hundred and fifty miles to Fort Griffin without running into trouble of some kind. Texas was too sparsely settled, and plagued by too many outlaws, to make any long journey, especially by a lone rider, safe. He'd just have to be ready when trouble found him.

Topper was eager to run, so after holding him to a walk until he warmed up, Vic allowed his paint to set his own pace. Topper broke into a gallop for half a mile, then slowed down to a mile eating lope. Eventually Topper settled into a steady trot.

Vic took it easy this first day out. He would cover about twenty-five miles until he reached Leander, where he would spend the night with Tom Puddicombe, a friend from his school days. He reached the town shortly after noon. Tom had only lived there a short time, so he had given Vic precise directions. Vic found Tom's home, a good-sized structure with a long front porch, neatly painted white with deep red shutters and trim, without any trouble. Tom was sitting in a cane backed rocker on the porch. He waved when Vic rode up.

"Howdy, Vic. It's been too long since we've seen each other."

"The Marshals Service keeps me real busy," Vic answered, as he got down from Topper. "How've you been, Tom?"

"I'm doing all right. Just taking life easy."

"Well, you've worked hard. You deserve time to relax and enjoy life."

"You hungry?"

"I could stand a bite."

"Good. I've got chili just about done, and home-brewed beer I've got on ice down in the root cellar. I'll tell you where to put your horse. He's a fine-looking animal, I might add. By the time he's cared for, the chili will be ready. We'll eat out here on the porch. You'll be able to put up your feet and set a spell."

"That sounds just fine. It's probably the last opportunity I'll have to relax for a long time."

"We can talk while we eat. The barn's around the back. There's a pump and sink in it you can use to clean up, after you get your horse settled. Don't worry about him getting along with Maisie, my carriage horse. She's a gentle soul."

"That sounds good."

Vic went around the back of the house, fed and groomed Topper, then washed up. Tom was still on the porch, but this time with a tray holding two heaping bowls of steaming chili, a loaf of bread, butter, and four bottles of beer on the wicker table in front of him.

"C'mon up and take a load off your feet, Vic,"

"I'll be more than happy to do just that."

He climbed the stairs to the porch, settled in a rocker next to Tom's.

Tom passed him a bowl of chili and bottle of beer.

Vic took a swig of beer, then a spoonful of chili.

"This is dang fine chili, old friend. The best I've had in a long time. Hot and spicy, but not blister your tongue and blow your ears off hot. Plenty of meat in it, too. Your own recipe?"

"Got it from my daughter Emma."

"Next time you see Emma give her my compliments."

"I'll be sure to do that."

"So, where are you off to this time?"

"Fort Griffin."

"Fort Griffin. Everyone knows that's a real dangerous town, a place to stay well clear of."

"I know. My job is to try'n clean it up. Make it a safer place for decent folks."

"By yourself?"

"By myself."

"Boy howdy, the Rangers are sure asking a lot from you. Fort Griffin needs a whole army to drive the renegades out."

"Tell me about it. I'll actually be up against the Army, which wants to declare martial law and take over the town. You know how well that would sit with us Texans."

"It wouldn't."

"That's right, it wouldn't. So I've got to keep the Army happy, along with taking on the buffalo hunters, gamblers, swindlers, and other assorted cutthroats infesting the town. My orders are to be diplomatic."

"Vic, I've never thought of you as being a diplomat."

"Neither has anyone else, including me. I don't know, perhaps after I get rid of some of the worst element I can calm things down. If not . . ."

Vic sighed, and shrugged his shoulders.

"Let's not worry about that tonight," Tom said. "Let's just sit here, enjoy the rest of the chili and beer, and palaver. We've got a lot of catching up to do."

"You're right," Vic agreed. "There's no use worrying until I reach Fort Griffin."

Vic and Tom talked well into the night, until the air, unusual for Austin in early summer, cooled enough to send them inside. After a good night's sleep, and a hearty breakfast of steak, eggs, biscuits and gravy, Vic saddled Topper and resumed his journey.

5

Vic rode steadily all day long, stopping on occasion to let Topper blow, making a longer stop for dinner at noon, where he let his paint have a drink from a shallow creek, then graze while Vic ate his lunch of bacon and biscuit sandwiches, which had been provided by Tom.

The route he was taking went mainly north by northwest. This section was on the eastern edge of the Hill Country. It traversed high plains for the most part, crossing some rolling hills and valleys. Vegetation was thick compared to much of Texas, with good grass, dotted with cactus, mesquite, various species of oak, and cottonwoods along the streams. As the days and miles went past and he drew nearer Fort Griffin, the terrain would level out, the vegetation changing more to prairie grasslands, with fewer trees and more dry country cactus and mesquite.

After covering more than fifty miles, Vic rode into the city of Lampasas, seat of the county of the same name. He and Topper were both dust-coated and weary, but still caught people's attention as they rode through the center of town.

Victor Vincent Verdugo was a native Texan, the son of a German woman whose family had emigrated to Mexico, and the upper-class

Mexican merchant she married. They had moved from Nuevo Laredo across the border to Laredo before Vic was born. He was their only child.

Orphaned at sixteen when his parents died of influenza, Vic was left to fend for himself. He was adrift until he signed on with the Texas Rangers during the Civil War. At the time the Rangers were a volunteer organization.

After the Confederacy was defeated, and the Rangers disbanded under Reconstruction, Vic wandered from one small town to another, acting as a deputy marshal. It was in one such town where he met a United States Marshal, who recruited him into the Marshals Service.

Vic had to walk a fine line between the Texans who still resented their loss in the war, and those who were trying to rebuild their lives.

Vic was a quiet man, not wasting words. At six foot two inches tall in his stocking feet, closer to six foot six in boots and high-crowned Stetson, when most men topped out at five foot eight or less, he didn't need to speak to get attention. He carried one hundred and ninety pounds of muscle on that six foot two frame.

Vic had strawberry blonde hair, and deep green eyes the color of emeralds. Those eyes could sparkle with merriment, or their sharp gaze could seem to bore right through any troublemakers. He wore a Smith and Wesson .44 American, one of the new and still rare cartridge revolvers, butt forward in a brown leather holster on his right hip for a left-handed cross draw, a draw that many claimed was even faster than the conventional draw.

For clothing, Vic favored an off-white Stetson, creased at the crown, the brim slightly upturned at the front, checked shirts, and denim trousers. His feet were encased in scuffed brown boots. Tied loosely around his neck was a royal blue silk wild rag.

Vic was a crack shot with that Smith and Wesson or the Winchester 1866 Yellowboy repeating rifle riding in a saddle scabbard under his right leg. He was deadly with his fists, and an expert at close in knife fighting. All in all, he was not a man to be trifled with.

Vic's horse Topper was a suitable match for the man, a horse that would stand out in any herd. Topper was a Medicine Hat paint, a mount widely prized by Indians, who believed its special markings granted its rider protection and strength in battle. Topper was almost pure white, except for the black "hat" across his ears and the top of his head, and a black "shield" covering his chest. Unusually, he had two blue or "glass" eyes, a feature which would make him even more valuable in any Indian's pony herd. He stood fifteen point three hands high, much taller than the average cow pony's height of around fourteen hands. With a deep chest and powerful legs, he had great speed and stamina, able to keep up a brutal pace for days on just snatches of grass, little water, and short rest. When Vic was in the saddle, he and Topper presented a formidable picture indeed.

Most distinct of all, Topper was still an intact stallion. The majority of men rode geldings, as stallions could be unpredictable, ornery, had a tendency to fight other horses, and call out to mares. The last trait being especially dangerous in outlaw territory. However, with Topper's gentle nature, except when in a running gun-battle or protecting his human partner, Vic had been unable to bring himself to cut his horse. Topper was naturally not a "talker", and with his innate intelligence he only needed a little training from Vic to remain quiet at all times, even when the scent of a mare in season was on the air. So instead of gelding him, Vic bred him to the mares of cowboys or ranchers who wanted to improve their stock, adding height, muscle, intelligence, stamina, speed and cow savvy to their herds. If a foal came out with the rare Medicine Hat markings, so much the better. And Vic made good use of the stud fees to supplement his meager Marshal's pay.

Knowing there were only two more towns after Lampasas, Brownwood and Cisco, both of which he intended to bypass, Vic decided to get a room for the night. His first chore was to find a stall for

Topper, since many livery stable owners refused to board stallions.

"There's a likely looking place just ahead, pard," Vic told Topper, after spying a sign which read "Lampasas Livery, Best Board at Reasonable rates." He kicked his horse into a slow jogtrot. A young man, of about twenty, tow-headed, skinny, wearing a faded red undershirt, denims one size too large held up by a pair of suspenders, and a flop-brimmed hat, sized up the horse and rider as they approached.

"Howdy, Mister. Lookin' to board that fine looking animal? Jody Hawkins. I run the best stable in Lampasas."

"Vic Verdugo. This here's Topper."

"Medicine Hat, huh? You don't see too many of those."

"No, you sure don't," Vic agreed. "Just to warn you, he's a stallion. Doesn't generally act studdy, though."

"That don't matter none. I've got a separate stall for stud hosses. It will cost you seventy-fives cents a day, though, rather than the usual fifty. Includes a bucket of grain tonight and in the morning, plenty of hay, and all the water he can drink. A good grooming, too, as long as he'll behave for that, being as he is a stud. He won't bite or kick, will he?"

"No, Topper's mostly gentle as a kitten," Vic said, as he dismounted. "The only thing that upsets him is if you bump his balls while you're working on his legs."

Hawkins laughed.

"I can't say as I blame him. I hate it when my balls get bumped, too."

Both men laughed.

"I reckon Topper's in good hands," Vic said. He gave Hawkins four quarters, told him to keep the change.

"Gee, thanks, Mister."

"It's Vic. Can you have him ready for me by seven tomorrow morning?"

"He'll have a full belly, a touch up brushing, and be waiting for you."

"That's fine. Topper, behave yourself tonight."

Topper nickered, rubbed his muzzle against Vic's shoulder.

"Of course I've got your candy."

Vic took a lemon drop from his shirt pocket, which Topper readily took. He handed the horse's reins to Hawkins.

"Just let me get my saddlebags and rifle, Jody. Also, can you tell me a good place to get a room, and also supper. Not too far a walk."

As did most men born to the saddle, Vic hated to walk, avoiding it if at all possible.

"Sure. The Lampasas Hotel is two blocks up on the left. Right across the street is Eve's Café. Eve serves up some mighty tasty chow. Besides the usual menu you see in most restaurants, she also has German food. And damn good beer. It's kept chilled, even in the summertime. I always tell folks passing through to eat at Eve's."

"Then that's what I'll do. I'm obliged, Jody. See you at seven tomorrow morning. Topper, you behave yourself."

Topper snorted and tossed his head, as if being insulted by the implication he wasn't always on his best behavior.

Vic shouldered his Winchester and saddlebags, then made the short walk to the hotel.

The lobby of the Lampasas was much like any frontier hotel, cleaner than most, but sparsely decorated, only a few chairs and tables scattered around a colorful rag rug. There were some landscape oils on the walls, potted plants on each end of the reception desk. The clerk was sound asleep in a cane-backed rocker behind the desk. He about jumped out of his skin when Vic banged on the bell.

"Huh? What?"

"Did I disturb your nap?" Vic asked, with a smile.

"I guess you did at that," the clerk admitted. "My apologies, sir."

"No need to apologize. I could use a good nap myself."

"Then you've come to the right place. The Lampasas is the finest lodging establishment in three counties. I'm William McKenzie, at your service. A room for tonight?"

"Yes, please."

"I have one here on the first floor, just off the lobby. Room 1. Will that do?"

"As long as it has a bed, it'll do just fine," Vic answered. "I'm on a long trip by horseback. Most of the rest of the way I'll be sleeping on the hard ground, with the sky for my roof. I intend to make the most of a comfortable bed and soft pillows tonight."

"I'm certain you'll find the accommodations more than satisfactory. The rate's a dollar a night. If you'll just sign the register, I'll give you your key."

"Of course."

Vic signed the proffered register and handed McKenzie a silver dollar.

McKenzie looked at Vic's signature, took a key from a pigeonhole and handed it to Vic.

"Here you go, Marshal. The room's on the right. If you need anything just let me know. I'll have Kenny, the boy who works for me, bring water, a pitcher and basin while you're at supper."

"I will, but a good meal and sleep is all I'm after. I'm going to wash up, then go over to Eve's for supper. The hostler at the livery suggested I sleep here and get a meal there."

McKenzie chuckled.

"Jody. He's right on both counts. Enjoy your stay, Marshal Verdugo."

"*Gracias*. I'm sure I will."

• • •

Vic's room was simply furnished, but spotlessly clean. He cleaned up and took a short nap. He then walked over to Eve's Café and *Biergarten.*

He was greeted by a buxom, blonde-haired blue-eyed woman in her late fifties when he stepped inside.

"*Willkommen.* I'm Eve Ekker. Welcome to my place. I hope you're hungry."

"I am. Starved, actually."

"You won't be when you leave here. I assure you of that. German food sticks to your ribs, and I don't skimp on the portions. *Bitte*, follow me."

She led Vic to a rear table in the half-filled room.

"Here is the menu. As you can see, our specialty is dishes from my native Bavaria. Our feature tonight is *sauerbraten mit knödeln.* To go with that I would suggest our home brewed German *bier*, a dark and hearty brew. *Lebkuchen mit schlagsahne* for dessert."

"That all sounds just fine," Vic answered.

"Excellent."

The meal was everything Eve Ekker promised, and more. Vic was stuffed by the time he finished. He had just paid the check and gotten up from his table when a young man came in.

The youngster was no more than seventeen, tow-headed and gray-eyed. He was hatless. A six-gun hung in a holster at his right hip. The look in his eyes was one Vic had seen all too often. The kid wanted to take down The Executioner, which, while that was the translation of Vic's surname into English, was also the nickname he'd been hung with and hated. He'd killed nowhere near as many men as the unwanted reputation he'd earned claimed. And all too often some young man who wanted to earn a reputation as a fast gun would challenge him to a duel.

The few patrons and Eve retreated to the back of the dining room, out of the line of fire.

"You Marshal Verdugo?" the kid challenged.

"That'd be me."

"I'm Kenny Davis, the *hombre* who's gonna kill you today, Marshal."

"The boy who works at the hotel?"

"That's right."

"Don't be a damn fool, boy. Just go on home to your ma and pa."

"I ain't no damn boy, Marshal. I'm a growed man. Faster on the draw than anyone else in these parts. I figure I'll plug you right in your damn belly. I want to see the look on your face when I put a slug into your damn guts."

"You're bound and determined to die today?"

"I ain't gonna die today, Marshal. You are."

"Then go for your gun whenever you're ready."

Vic's left hand hovered over the butt of the Colt on his right hip, ready to pull the Peacemaker in a blindingly fast cross draw. His green eyes seemed to turn the color of the stormy North Atlantic Ocean.

Kenny started to sweat when Vic's gaze seemed to bore a hole clean through him. He swallowed hard when Vic started to walk toward him, one slow step at a time.

"I'm waitin', kid. Pull your iron."

Kenny's hand, which he had about four inches over the butt of his pistol, lowered about an inch, then hesitated.

"What's the matter? You yella? You said you were gonna kill me. What are you waiting for?"

Vic kept walking toward the boy, locking his gaze with Kenny. The sweat was now streaking the boy's face. His chin quivered.

"C'mon, kid. Pull that gun. Sink that bullet into my guts. You ever killed a man before, or even seen one die? It's not a pretty sight, especially a man who's been gut-shot. He dies real slow, whining and crying in pain. Blood everywhere."

"I . . . I . . ."

Vic was near enough to stop Kenny without gunplay. He lunged for him, grabbed his right wrist, and slapped him twice across the face. The boy started sobbing.

"You should've killed me, Marshal, rather than shaming me."

"Now why would I want to do that? And why would you want to die?"

"Because . . . because."

"You don't want to die for no reason, like challenging a man to a gunfight," Vic said, empathy in his voice. "Even if you'd somehow managed to gun me down tonight, sooner or later someone would come along who'd be faster than you. Then you'd be dead, and proved what? Nothing. Your embarrassment will pass, but death doesn't. It's final. Do you have a family?"

"Yes. My ma and pa, two little brothers and four little sisters."

"Think about how they would have felt if you'd died in a stupid gunfight, just for your damn pride. Now go on home."

"You're not gonna take my gun, Marshal?"

"No, long as you promise me you won't use it except when necessary, not to try and prove something."

"I've learned my lesson. Thanks, Marshal."

"*Por nada*."

Once Kenny left, Eve walked over to Vic.

"You handled that real well, Marshal. It would have been a shame if you'd had to kill him. He's really not a bad boy. Just has to learn how to be a man. He learned something tonight. Let's just hope it sticks."

"I think it will. I'll see you for breakfast."

"I'm looking forward to it."

6

Vic made good progress over the next two days, covering nearly half of the remaining one hundred sixty miles to Fort Griffin. On his second day out from Lampasas, Topper kept pinning back his ears and rolling his eyes, along with snorting and tossing his head.

"I know, boy," Vic said to the paint, patting his shoulder. "I'm aware there's two men back there trailing us. They've been following us ever since we passed through Goldthwaite. Keeping the same distance between us, and stopping whenever we stop. I don't think they've realized we're onto them, but I can't be certain. It's only about an hour until sundown. We'll make camp just after dusk, see what they do. And thanks for the warning, pardner. You'll get an extra lemon drop tonight."

The trail had edged more into the northeast corner of the Hill Country. The terrain wasn't as rugged as in most of that region, but not as flat as the past forty miles. It consisted of low rolling hills and valleys, the vegetation a mixture of grasslands and mesquite scrub, along with trees such as juniper and several species of oaks.

Vic rode for another ninety minutes, then turned Topper into a narrow valley between two low ridges. A small spring seeped from where the ridges joined, forming a steep wall which dead-ended the valley. Cottonwoods and willows surrounded the waterhole.

"This is perfect for our purposes, Topper," Vic said, as he dismounted. "If those sons of bitches trailing us are planning a drygulching, which I'm certain they are, they won't be able to get around behind us. They can only come in the same way we did. There's grass for you, water for both of us. Let me get you rubbed down, then we can both eat while we wait for our guests."

Vic pulled the gear off Topper, setting the saddle upright, draping the saddle blanket over it to dry, placing the bridle on the ground next to it. He took the currycomb and hoof pick from his saddlebags, cleaning the dirt and sweat out of his horse's hide and digging dirt and pebbles from his hooves.

After Topper was cared for, Vic picketed him to graze. He turned to his own needs. He gathered fallen branches to build a fire, piled them up, then took bacon, beans, and flour from his saddlebags, along with a small frying pan and coffee pot.

He lit the fire, mixed flour and water for fry bread, added the dough to the bacon and beans already sizzling in the pan, then put coffee and water in the pot to boil.

Once the food was done, Vic settled down cross-legged on the ground to eat his supper.

He avoided gazing into the fire, since that could cause brief blindness, which might prove fatal if the men following him approached before his vision readjusted to the darkness.

Vic had built his fire larger than usual, making it easy to spot. That would give the impression he was a greenhorn, new to the territory, without the knowledge that, to stay safe in untamed territory, you made a small, almost smokeless fire. Some nights it was necessary to not build a fire at all, in order to avoid unwanted visitors.

Vic was halfway through his meal when Topper stopped grazing. The Medicine Hat lifted his head, neck arched and ears pricked sharply forward. His nostrils flared as he keened the air. He gave a soft snuffle. His actions told Vic someone was approaching as plainly as if the horse could speak.

Vic set down his plate, pulled the Smith and Wesson from its holster, and held it in his lap. He could now hear the soft hoof steps of slowly approaching horses. Now it was time to wait.

Soon, the hoof steps went silent. A voice called from outside the circle of firelight.

"Hello, the fire. Is it all right if we come on in?"

"If you're friendly, ride on in," Vic answered. "Slow and easy, though, until I can get a good look at you. How many?"

"Two of us," the same voice answered.

A moment later, the men emerged from the darkness. One was on a bay, the other a sorrel. The same color horses the men who'd been following Vic rode.

"Do you mind if we get down?" one asked.

"Not at all. I've still got some bacon and beans left, along with some coffee, if you're hungry."

"Why, that's right kindly of you, Mister. My name's Bill. Pardner is Dekotha. We could stand a bite to eat. We're new to this territory, hadn't found a good place to make camp for the night. We saw your fire, and were hoping we'd be welcome."

As he often did when not wanting to be recognized, Vic used the short form of his middle name when he answered.

"Vince. Light and set. Help yourselves to some grub. I ain't the best cook, but I ain't the worst, neither."

"We're obliged."

The pair dismounted, and tied their horses to one of the cottonwoods. Vic noticed they didn't offer the mounts, which had to be thirsty and hungry, the opportunity to drink or graze. The animals were forced to settle for nibbling on the cottonwood's leaves and twigs.

The man who called himself Bill was tall and lean, with shoulder length brown hair and light brown eyes. He was dressed all in denim, except for the red silk bandanna around his neck, and the black hat on his head. A revolver was in the holster hanging at his right hip.

Dekotha appeared to be a half-breed. He had the black hair and high cheekbones of an Indian, probably a Kiowa, but his eyes were a deep gray, his skin lighter than a full-blooded Native, indicating white blood in his ancestry. He also had a revolver at his right hip, a bone handled knife in a beaded and fringed sheath on his left. His clothes were buckskin, the shirt fringed across the chest. His hat was a bowler, with three eagle feathers stuck in the band. It made an incongruous contrast to the rest of his outfit.

They pulled tin plates, mugs, and forks from their saddlebags. After filling the plates and mugs, they settled cross-legged on the ground, about fifteen feet opposite Vic, one to his right, the other to his left.

They're gonna try for me all right, Vic thought. *Settin' up to catch me in a crossfire. Just have to be ready when they pull their guns.*

"This is mighty fine grub," Bill said, as he scooped beans into his mouth. "Ain't it, Dekotha? I said, ain't it?"

Dekotha grunted.

"It's not half bad," he muttered.

Vic had long ago learned how to read men's eyes, their slightest motions. It was how he stayed alive in his dangerous chosen profession, where a man's lifespan was measured in months, not years.

Both of the men finished eating at the same time. They stood up, dropped their plates, and grabbed for their guns.

Vic lifted his American from his lap, aimed it at Bill, and shot him in the gut. He shifted the pistol, thumbed back the hammer, and put a bullet just above Dekotha's groin. He put a second slug into the man's chest, then turned his gun back on Bill, who was still standing, staggering toward Vic while trying to get his gun level. Vic shot him again, this time sinking a bullet into his stomach.

Bill jackknifed, dropped to his knees, then fell to his face. Dekotha was lying on his side, legs bent, one arm outstretched, the other along his side and hip, the gun still in his hand.

Vic still had three bullets left in his gun. He got up, walked over to Dekotha. Blood stained the crotch of the half-breed's pants, and a crimson stain spread over his shirtfront. Dekotha gave out one last, ragged gasp, then his breathing stopped. Vic pulled the gun from his hand, and shoved it behind his own waistband.

Vic went over to Bill, using the toe of his boot to roll the lanky gunman onto his back.

Bill was still alive. His eyes were glassy, his breathing labored. He managed to press one hand to the bullet hole low in his gut, the other covered the hole in his stomach.

He glared at Vic.

"Damn. You done kilt . . . me, mister. Dekotha?"

"Your pard's already dead."

"You . . . got us . . . both? Damn . . . We figured . . . you were . . . an easy mark. And Dekotha sure had his mind set on that Medicine Hat horse of yours. It was the Kiowa in him."

"You figured wrong. I'm a Deputy United States Marshal. Victor Verdugo. I've known you two have been following me ever since Goldthwaite. I was ready for anything y'all tried to pull off."

Bill's eyes widened in surprise.

"The Executioner? No wonder you outgunned us both."

"Some folks call me that, yeah. I'm not particularly fond of havin' that title hung on me."

"And we picked . . . you as a . . . target. Damn fools . . . we were. Man, my guts burn like . . . they're on fire."

He choked on the blood filling his mouth, shuddered. His body stiffened, then went slack, his eyes wide open in the unblinking stare of death.

Vic sighed.

"Now I've got to haul these bodies into Brownwood," he muttered to himself. "I'm purely tempted to just leave these two here for the scavengers, but there might be warrants for them."

Topper let out a loud whinny.

"I'm fine, boy," Vic called. "Go back to eating, or sleeping, or whatever you were doing. I've got some work to finish before I can turn in."

First he took the gear off the dead men's horses, untied them, let them have all the water they wanted, then picketed them where they could graze. He then took the bedrolls from the saddles, and used the blankets to wrap the corpses, which he dragged to the side of the clearing. He washed out the dishes, including those of the gunmen, and stacked them alongside the spring. Those chores done, he rolled and smoked a cigarette, then unrolled his own blankets and slid under them. Within fifteen minutes, he was fast asleep.

7

Vic lost nearly half a day in Brownwood. It turned out the men who'd tried to ambush him were William Hollis and Dekotha Sanchez, both of whom had outstanding warrants for horse thieving and assault in Nebraska, New Mexico Territory, and Arkansas. He had to leave the bodies with the Brown County Coroner, fill out two copies of a report on the incident, file one with the Brown County Sheriff, and mail one back to Austin. He also sent a telegram to Judge Canton, explaining the progress he had made so far, telling him about the failed ambush, and advising the judge he would reach Fort Griffin the following night.

By the time he left the Western Union office, it was close to noon, so he crossed the street and ate dinner at a small café. He stopped at the general store to pick up a few supplies, a box of extra cartridges for his six-gun and shells for his rifle, some beef jerky, a sack of Bull Durham smoking tobacco and cigarette papers for himself, a sack of lemon drops and a small sack of grain for Topper. The horse would enjoy that for his supper tonight. It was shortly after one when he rode out of Brownwood.

With nearly one hundred miles still ahead of

him, Vic didn't push his horse. He traveled about fifty miles, the light of the almost full moon illuminating the trail, easing the effort of riding after the sun went down. He stopped for the night about eleven o'clock alongside a shallow creek. After unsaddling Topper, he poured out the sack of oats, which the big horse ate with gusto. Vic ate half of the jerky he'd purchased, washing it down with water from his canteen, then refilling the vessel with creek water. After finishing his supper, he rolled and smoked a quirly. The night was warm, so Vic didn't bother with a fire, nor taking his bedroll from the saddle. He simply stretched out on his back in the soft grass, using his saddle for a pillow.

Who knows. I'll be in Fort Griffin by tomorrow. This could be the last peaceful night of sleep I'll get for a long time.

He gazed up at the sky, saying a silent prayer as he watched the moon work its way toward the western horizon. He was still praying when slumber claimed him.

8

Two hours before dusk, Vic found a secluded spot about ten miles south of Fort Griffin, well off the main trail. He turned Topper into it, dismounted and let the horse graze, leaving the saddle on, cinches tight, and bridle in place.

"We're gonna wait here until after dark, Topper," he told his horse. "I want to take a *pasear* around the place before we get down to business, see if it's as rough a town as its reputation. Since we have to go by the Army fort to reach town, I don't want to run across any soldiers who might stop and question us. We'll also get a better idea of what we're up against at night. That's when the rowdies come out."

Topper rubbed his velvety muzzle against Vic's chest.

"I'm sorry, pal. I know it's not all that comfortable having to eat with the cinches tight around your belly and needing to work the grass around the bit in your mouth, but if trouble comes up I won't have the time to saddle and bridle you. It's just for a short while. You eat while I catch some shut-eye."

While Topper fell to cropping the grass, Vic settled under the shade of a good-sized cottonwood. He sat with his back against the tree's trunk, rolled and smoked a quirly, finished it and pulled his hat low over his face. He started musing about the town he'd been assigned to tame.

Fort Griffin itself was on the top of a plateau, which overlooked a bend of the Clear Fork of the Brazos River. The post had first been named Fort Wilson, then renamed in honor of General Charles Griffin, who had died during a yellow fever epidemic in Galveston.

The town of Fort Griffin sprang up on the bottomlands between the fort and the river. It was sometimes called The Bottom, The Flat, or Hide Town, the last due to the many buffalo hunters who frequented the town. The Great Western Cattle Trail ran from San Antonio north through Fort Griffin to Dodge City, Kansas. The hundreds of cowboys tending the herds, buffalo hunters, and the black and white soldiers from the fort made a volatile mixture. Add in the gamblers, card sharps, con artists, thieves, killers and prostitutes who frequented towns such as Fort Griffin meant trouble was a constant threat. Since the owners and clients of the saloons, gambling houses, and brothels wouldn't want law and order to be established, cutting down on their business, any lawman would not be welcomed with open arms, to put things mildly.

It was into this boiling witch's cauldron that Vic was about to ride.

• • •

Vic waited until after nine o'clock before he rode into Fort Griffin, allowing time for the town to really get roaring. The fort itself was deceptively quiet as he rode past it and down the slope to town, but even at this distance the noise of the men crowding the streets and businesses established for their entertainment could be heard.

Vic rode through Fort Griffin's single main street, which had hastily thrown together buildings of raw lumber built haphazardly on each side. There were even still a few tent saloons in place, their "bars" simply wood planks set up on empty whiskey barrels. The entire town appeared as if a good stiff wind would blow it out of existence.

Two men, buffalo hunters by their appearance, rolled out of a saloon just as Vic rode by. Topper had to sidestep the men, who were grappling each other in a fierce fistfight. They got to their feet, one holding a long-bladed bone handled knife. He shoved the knife hilt deep into his opponent's belly, twisted it, then yanked it out. The wounded man howled with pain, clamped his left hand to his ripped open gut in a futile attempt to shove back in place a section of protruding intestine. He dropped to his knees, pulled an ancient Colt Dragoon from behind his greasy buffalo hide shirt, and shot the man who'd stabbed him. The bullet penetrated the man's chest and lodged in his heart. Both men fell face down in the manure and dirt of the street. No one paid any attention, merely walked around the bodies to wherever they were headed.

Vic kept Topper moving. Two blocks on, a man ran out of an alleyway, lunged at him, grabbed Topper's reins and attempted to shove Vic out of the saddle. Vic pulled his left foot from the stirrup and kicked the man squarely in the face, flattening his nose and snapping his head back. The man dropped like a rock. Vic didn't look back to see if he'd broken the would-be horse thief's neck or not. He just put Topper into a trot, leaving the man sprawled in the middle of the road.

Vic patted Topper's neck.

"So far, this has been some welcome to this Hell on Earth, bud. We're gonna have our work cut out for us. I've seen enough for tonight. I'll find a stable for you and get a room for myself. First thing tomorrow morning we'll head up to the fort and request a meeting with the commanding officer."

Close to what could be considered the center of town stood one of the few substantial looking structures, a two-story wooden building. A sign hanging from it proclaimed *The Occidental Hotel*, in a florid red script, the color already beginning to fade to rose under the merciless Texas sun. A sign attached to the side of the hotel read *Livery Stable. Horses Boarded and Rented.* The lettering was black, but an arrow pointing down the alleyway between the hotel and the Beehive Saloon was done in the same red as the hotel's sign.

"I reckon we've found our stop for the night, Topper."

Vic turned his horse into the alley. At its far end stood a ramshackle, unpainted barn, with corrals to either side. Two wall lanterns on each side of the door threw dim light into the alley.

Vic rode up to the barn, dismounted, and knocked on the door. It swung open a moment later, to reveal a black man of indeterminate age, anywhere from forty to sixty. He was bald, but had a thick gray beard. He wore a red wool undershirt, denims held up by one suspender at his right hip, no hat, and well-worn work boots.

"Can I help you, Mister?" he asked, revealing a mouth missing most of its teeth.

"I hope so. I need a stall for my horse. Just to warn you, he's a stallion. Behaves like a gelding though, even around the mares."

"I've got a corral with a lean-to shed. Will that do?"

"It might. Long as no one tries to steal him."

"You must be new to Fort Griffin. Anything that's not nailed down is liable to be stolen. Even some things that are. A whole shack just up and disappeared one night."

He took a closer look at Topper.

"And a horse like yours is a prime target for any horse thief or prowling Indian. One of those damn Comanches or Kiowas will sneak into town on occasion, looking to steal horses or firewater. I'll do my best to keep him here, but no promises."

"One question before I decide. Do you happen to know if the hotel up the alley has any rooms available?"

"The Occidental? It owns this here stable. I work for them. If I have room for a horse, they have room for that horse's owner."

The hostler stopped and chuckled.

"Even if they were full up, it wouldn't take long for a room to become available. Someone'd either get thrown out or shot. Most likely both."

"That sure sounds like I won't get much sleep."

"After about four in the morning you might. Now what's it gonna be? You gonna leave your horse here or not?"

"I reckon it's as safe a place as any," Vic answered. "What's the rate?"

"How long you gonna need the corral?"

"I don't rightly know yet."

"For hotel guests it's fifty cents a night, or six-fifty a week. That includes grain twice a day, water, and hay. Also grooming, unless you prefer to do that yourself."

"I do, except I'd be obliged if you'd rub him

down tonight for me. I've had a long ride, and I'm tired. Let's figure on two weeks for now."

"Sure. I'm Elijah Watts. Your name?"

"Vic. Vic Verdugo. My horse is named Topper."

"I can see why. Any Indian would be sure proud to count coup on you, take your scalp and that Medicine Hat."

"A few have tried. They died for the effort."

"You're a big man. Just don't get too uppity. Fort Griffin will cut you down to size."

"I don't plan on letting that happen."

Vic pulled out his billfold, handed Elijah a ten-dollar yellowback, then reached in his pocket, took out a five-dollar half eagle gold coin, and gave that to him.

"The change is for you, Elijah."

"Why, thank you, Mister Verdugo. Thank you a heap."

"Vic."

He handed Topper's reins to the liveryman.

"Just let me get my saddlebags and rifle before you take him."

Vic untied his saddlebags, shouldered them, removed his Winchester from its boot and carried it in his left hand.

"Topper, you go with Elijah here."

"We'll get along just fine, won't we, Topper?"

Elijah ran a gentle hand down the horse's neck and shoulder. Topper snuffled.

"Elijah, I'll need him about seven-thirty tomorrow

morning. Can you have him ready for me? Just fed. I'll saddle him myself."

"He'll be ready and waiting."

"*Gracias. Buenos noches.*"

"Good night."

The Occidental Hotel didn't look any more appealing on its interior than its exterior. As were the outside walls, the lobby was unpainted, gaps between the planks where the raw lumber had shrunk and warped. The reception desk was also plain wood, unvarnished. There was no bank of pigeonholes behind the desk, only nails in the wall holding the room keys. The floor was rough and splintery, no paintings hung on the walls to add life to the room. A single coal oil lamp in the center of the ceiling, and another on the desk, provided the only illumination. No chairs were provided, indicating the hotel owners didn't want anyone loitering in the lobby. Considering Fort Griffin's well-deserved reputation, Vic really couldn't blame them.

The man behind the desk appeared as rough a character as many of the men Vic encountered during his ride through Fort Griffin. He was about five foot eight, lantern jawed and scruffy-bearded, with a blocky, powerful build. Weighing about two hundred pounds, few if any of those pounds fat. His shoulder length hair was dark brown, his eyes the same hue. There was a knife scar which ran from the center of his forehead and over his left eyebrow, curving to end in the middle of his left cheek. It came so close to his left eye the eye was half-closed in a permanent squint. He wore an ill-fitting white shirt with black sleeve garters and dark gray trousers, the top three buttons of the shirt undone, revealing a chest covered with thick black hair, which made the clothes look even more incongruous. He eyed Vic with a look of indifference.

"Howdy. I'm looking for a room."

"Most people who come in here are. How long do you plan on staying?"

"I'll start off with two weeks. Could be longer."

"The rate's two dollars a night, in advance. Includes nothing but a bed, basin, and a pitcher of water. No soap or towels. No change of sheets during your stay. Outhouses are behind the building."

"That's awfully expensive for poor accommodations," Vic answered.

"This is the only hotel in town. Take it or leave it."

"I reckon I'll take it."

"You'll have room six. Pay me and sign the register."

Vic took a ten-dollar bill and four silver dollars from his left vest pocket. He handed them to the clerk, who bit the coins to make certain they were genuine, then turned the register for Vic to sign.

Vic hesitated just a moment before scrawling his signature across the page.

Time to let them know there's a new marshal in town.

He wrote *Victor V. Verdugo, United States Deputy Marshal* with a flourish.

When he turned the register back around, the desk clerk stared wide-eyed at him.

"Here's your key, Marshal. Room's just down the hallway."

"*Gracias, amigo.*"

Vic took the key.

That worked. By tomorrow morning half of Fort Griffin will know there's a United States Deputy Marshal here. With luck word will even get back to the fort.

He found Room 6, turned the key in the flimsy lock. The ill-fitted door swung open of its own accord. The clerk's description had understated how shabby the room truly was. The lone single bed was covered with yellowed sheets and a thin, ratty blanket. A single bedside stand held a grimy lamp. In the corner was a rickety stand holding a chipped basin and cracked pitcher. The gaps in the walls were wide enough he could see into each of the adjoining rooms. He shook his head as he locked the door, and muttered in disgust as he looked around more closely.

"Here's hoping I won't have any noisy neighbors. And that door sure as hell won't stop anybody who might decide to break in here. Well, it's only for a couple of weeks at most. After I visit the fort, I'll take some time to find better lodging. I'll be here quite a while, unless I miss my guess."

Vic didn't bother to pull back the sheets. The mattress was undoubtedly infested with fleas and lice. Lying atop the sheets would offer at least some meager protection from those blood thirsty parasites. He went to bed fully dressed, not even removing his boots or gun belt. He removed his Smith and Wesson from its holster, put a bullet into the empty chamber under the hammer, and placed it within easy reach. Lying on his back, he took his rosary from his vest pocket and began fingering the beads as he recited the prayer. Once done, he placed the rosary atop his pistol, and was immediately asleep.

9

When Vic rode through Fort Griffin the following morning, the town seemed completely different. Few people were on the streets, although trash was strewn everywhere. The bodies of the dead buffalo hunters were nowhere in sight, nor the man whom Vic had kicked unconscious, or dead, when he tried to steal Topper. Vic knew the peace and quiet was only an illusion. The denizens of towns like Fort Griffin slept until well into the day. The town would only begin to awake around noon, and not come fully alive until night fell.

Vic continued through town and rode up the hill to Fort Griffin itself. Many of the fort's buildings were still only half completed, stone foundations and partially built stone walls topped with vertically placed logs or earth, many with canvas stretched over them for makeshift roofs.

When Vic rode up to what passed for the main gate, the buffalo soldier on sentry duty stopped him. He looked at the Deputy Marshal's shield pinned to Vic's chest.

"State your business, Marshal."

"Deputy United States Marshal Victor Verdugo.

I'm here to meet with Colonel Martin Elliott."

"Do you have an appointment with the colonel, sir?"

"No, I'm afraid I don't. I only arrived in town last night. I'm hoping he can allow me a few minutes to speak with him. If he can't right now, I'll ask for an appointment while I'm here."

"Would you please show me some identification, sir?"

"Of course."

Vic took out his billfold, opened it, and removed his commission papers, which he handed to the soldier.

"These seem to be in order, sir," he said, after examining the papers. "You may proceed. The Headquarters building is straight ahead. It's the only one that's completely finished."

"Thank you, Corporal."

Vic heeled Topper into a walk. He was surprised at how neat and tidily kept the post was, especially an uncompleted post on the Texas frontier. Soldiers were busy at various tasks, cleaning up the grounds, working on buildings, or tending to horses. The ringing of a hammer on an anvil came from the blacksmith shop. He reached the Headquarters building, dismounted, and tied Topper to the hitchrail.

"I don't know how long I'll be," he told the horse. "Here's something to tide you over."

He gave Topper two lemon drops, which the

horse eagerly took, happily crunching down on them.

Vic climbed the stairs and went inside. A lieutenant was at a desk in the small lobby, working on a stack of papers. He looked up when Vic walked in.

"How might I help you?"

"Deputy United States Marshal Victor Verdugo. I've been assigned to Fort Griffin. Just got into town last night. I'd like to ask Colonel Elliott for a few minutes of his time."

"I'm the colonel's adjutant. I'm afraid he has a very busy schedule."

"Would you kindly at least ask him, Lieutenant . . . ?"

"Stanton. Jeremiah Stanton."

"Then would you please ask the colonel? It will only take you a moment or two. I also promise I won't take up more of his time than absolutely necessary."

Stanton sighed. The look on his face made it clear he'd like to be rid of this bothersome deputy marshal. However, it was obvious the man wouldn't leave until his request was met.

"All right."

He got up and disappeared into a rear office. He returned with a look of surprise on his face.

"Colonel Elliott says he can give you thirty minutes."

"That will be fine. Thank you."

"Follow me, please."

Vic followed Stanton to Elliott's office. The room was decorated with Elliott's many commissions, promotions, and commendations. Most prominently displayed was Elliott's diploma from West Point. Two crossed sabers hung under that.

"Colonel, this is Deputy United States Marshal Victor Verdugo. Marshal, Colonel Elliott."

"You're dismissed, Lieutenant. Close the door behind you."

"Yes, sir!" Stanton gave Elliott a stiff salute, then went back to his desk.

Colonel Elliott was standing. He was a tall man, five foot ten or so, about one hundred and eighty pounds. He had brown hair, graying at the temples and cropped short, hazel eyes, and a pencil thin moustache. His uniform was clean and neatly pressed, a number of campaign medals pinned to the left breast. He carried himself with the military bearing of a career officer, his posture ramrod straight. He didn't offer to shake Vic's hand, nor offer him any coffee or a cigar.

"Good morning, Marshal. Please, have a seat."

"Thank you, Colonel."

Vic sat in a wooden armchair opposite Elliott's desk. The colonel sat down, leaned forward, put his elbows on the desk and tented his hands.

"Lieutenant Stanton informs me you have been assigned to the town of Fort Griffin. You are aware this comes as a total surprise to me."

"I wasn't positive, since word often leaks out, but that is as it was supposed to be."

"Might I ask what your specific orders are?"

"Politely, to bring law and order to Fort Griffin. More bluntly, to clean up the whole damn town, and run the bad elements out of the place."

"I see. Are you aware I have requested that martial law be declared in Fort Griffin, so that it would be placed under control of the Army?"

"I am."

"And . . ."

"With all due respect, I am the answer to that request, Colonel. My orders were issued by Judge Isaiah Canton, the Chief Federal Justice for the State of Texas."

"The Army has the right to declare martial law under Reconstruction," Elliott snapped.

"Colonel, you are well aware Reconstruction is coming to an end. The last thing needed is to stir up resentment among Texans again by subjugating them to Federal control any longer."

"I take it you are a Texan, sir!"

"I am," Vic confirmed, "but I'm no Confederate. I spent the war as a Texas Ranger, defending settlers from mostly Indian raids, but also Mexican outlaws, black desperadoes, and white renegades and deserters from both North and South. I was recruited into the Marshals Service after the war concluded."

"I don't like the idea of a deputy marshal

riding into my jurisdiction and taking over."

"Your jurisdiction is the fort, not the town, Colonel. The Army is here to protect settlers from Indian raids. Enforcing civilian law is up to local or state authorities, or United States Marshals. Is that clear?"

"It is. However, I will be writing to Washington, filing an official protest and requesting your orders be rescinded. Also, you can expect no help from me or any Army personnel. I don't imagine you'll last more than a month in any event before running away with your tail between your legs, or more likely dead. Taming Fort Griffin is a job for more than one man."

"You've stated your position clearly, Colonel. I'm not asking for any assistance, except this. If any of your soldiers, black or white, officer or enlisted man, commits a crime in town, they will be arrested and confined. They'll be tried in a civilian court, unless it is a soldier-on-soldier offense, in which case, they will be remanded to your custody for court-martial."

"You can't do that!"

"I can, and I will. I've said my piece. Do you have anything more to add?"

"I don't believe so, no."

"Then I'll let you get back to your work, with a warning. Stay out of my way. I won't interfere in military affairs, and I will brook no interference in mine. I'll see my way out."

Vic got up and stalked out, slamming the door behind him, leaving Elliott staring at it.

"I believe the colonel wants to see you now, Lieutenant," Vic told the adjutant.

Stanton jumped up and scurried down the hallway like a frightened rabbit.

Vic chuckled as he untied Topper, who nuzzled him and whickered a question.

"No, pard, I don't think I acted like a diplomat in there. I'm certain Judge Canton wouldn't be very happy with me right about now. Let's get back to town."

Vic mounted, turned the paint from the rail, and put him into a slow lope.

10

Vic returned to the town itself. Unlike the previous night, when he'd ridden in with his badge out of sight, today it was in plain sight, glittering in the sun. Most everyone noticed him. People pointed him out, murmuring or whispering to each other. He could feel them staring at his broad back. That didn't bother him, as long as those stares weren't followed by a bullet or two into aforesaid back. That would indeed upset him. Not that it would matter, because he'd be beyond knowing or caring. He'd be dead.

Vic's first stop was at the town's newspaper, the *Fort Griffin Echo.* The green-eyeshade-wearing young man setting type greeted him warmly when he walked in.

"Howdy, mister. I'll be with you as soon as I get this type locked in place. If I leave it now it's liable to spill all over the floor, which means I'll have to start all over."

"I'm in no particular hurry."

Vic found a chair and settled down to peruse a week-old copy of the *Echo.* It contained a few advertisements, two legal notices, some business news, and a "running list" of the number of shootings, assaults, and violent deaths in Fort Griffin since the first of the year. He'd just finished when the apparent publisher left his work, wiping his ink-stained hands on an even more ink-stained apron. He saw the badge Vic wore.

"Howdy, Marshal. I'd heard rumors there was a new lawman come to town. I have to say I'm real happy to see you. Dale Sullivan."

Sullivan was an earnest looking man in his early twenties, sandy haired and gray eyed, of average height and weight.

He offered Vic his hand, which Vic took. Sullivan had a grip almost as firm as his own.

"Sorry about the ink."

"It's not any problem. Victor Verdugo. I go by Vic."

"What might I do for you, Marshal?"

"I need some handbills printed. Say about a dozen."

"Of course. What will they say?"

"Let me have a pencil and paper. I'll write out the copy."

"Sure."

Sullivan went to a cluttered table, picked up a pencil and sheet of paper. He handed those to Vic.

"Here you are."

"Thanks."

Vic carefully printed out the words he wanted all of Fort Griffin to see. He handed the sheet to Sullivan, who read it silently.

NOTICE:

PER ORDER OF THE HONORABLE ISAIAH CANTON, CHIEF FEDERAL JUSTICE FOR THE STATE OF TEXAS, UNITED STATES, DEPUTY MARSHAL VICTOR V. VERDUGO HAS BEEN ASSIGNED TO ESTABLISH AND MAINTAIN LAW AND ORDER IN THE TOWN OF FORT GRIFFIN, TEXAS, AND ITS ENVIRONS.

ANY CRIME OR INFRACTION, NO MATTER HOW SMALL, SHALL BE PUNISHABLE BY FINE, IMPRISONMENT, OR DEATH BY HANGING.

RESISTING ARREST WILL NOT BE TOLERATED, AND THE PERPETRATOR WILL BE SUBJECT TO BEING SHOT WITHOUT WARNING.

VICTOR V. VERDUGO
UNITED STATES DEPUTY MARSHAL
DISTRICT OF TEXAS

"Whooee! This'll sure stir things up," Sullivan said. "It's high time something was done about the out-of-control crime in this town. I do have one question. Fort Griffin has no jail. Where do you intend to imprison anyone?"

"I'm still working on that," Vic answered. "I

haven't even looked for a place for my office yet, let alone a jail."

"The Army has a stockade they're not making much use of. Perhaps Colonel Elliott would allow you use of it."

"The colonel and I didn't exactly hit it off."

"I'm not surprised, Marshal. He doesn't seem to care what his soldiers do in town, but let a civilian so much as look at him the wrong way and he wants that person thrown in irons. He's bound and determined to have martial law declared in Fort Griffin so he can take control of the town."

"Which is why he wasn't happy to see me show up."

"I can imagine. How soon do you want the handbills?"

"As quickly as possible."

"I can get to work on them as soon as I get the paper printed. Of course, I now have to change the front page. The headline story will be your arrival, Marshal. I hope you don't mind. My editorial will support you. As far as the handbills, late this afternoon."

"The First Amendment says even if I did, which I don't, I have no right to stop you from printing it."

"Excellent. Will you give me a statement?"

"Just this. The reign of robberies, killings, and lesser crimes in Fort Griffin is about to come to an end. I have sworn to make that happen."

"Succinct and to the point. Perfect. I hope you realize a lot of the business owners in town will be against you. They rely on liquor, gambling, and prostitution for their money. You're about to upset the applecart."

"If you print that they're also liable to come after you."

"They've already threatened that. I don't take kindly to threats, nor do I back down from a fight."

"Good. Dale, I doubt I'll make many friends in this town. I hope I can count on you as one."

"You can, Marshal."

"Vic."

Vic's next stop was Foster's Hardware Store, where he purchased forty-eight ten penny nails and a sturdy hammer. Bertram Hawks Foster, the owner, was reluctant to sell them to the Marshal, fearing repercussions from some of the other business owners. Vic convinced him not selling him the nails would result in much more severe repercussions.

Until the handbills were ready, Vic strolled around Fort Griffin, making his presence known. He stopped in at the Wong Fong Chinese restaurant for lunch. The owner eyed him with trepidation, his hands shaking as he placed Vic's order on the counter. Vic couldn't tell if the man was terrified of him, or the less than savory denizens of the town.

After eating, he continued his walk-through, noting the likely places where trouble would start, the saloons, gambling parlors, brothels, and others of their ilk.

One particularly bold prostitute sashayed up to Vic and offered him her services, in broad daylight on the main street. When Vic turned her down, she cursed him out in some very unladylike language. Vic chuckled as he walked away.

By three o'clock, Sullivan had the handbills ready. Vic went through town, nailing them to walls and posts at prominent places where they would be most seen. He made certain a number of them were posted on saloons and gambling dens. He turned around at a shout from behind him. A man dressed in bartender's clothes was holding the handbill he'd just hung next to the doors of the Big Bob's saloon. Two other men, dressed in range clothes, were on either side of him. They had a sinister look about them. Both already had their hands hovering over the butts of their revolvers.

"Hey, Marshal. Did you just hang this here poster on my business?"

"I did," Vic answered. He dropped the handbills he still carried. "I don't appreciate your taking it down, neither."

"I'll show you what I think of it."

The saloonkeeper tore the handbill to shreds, throwing the pieces into the dirt and grinding them under his heel.

Vic's eyes gleamed like the sun reflecting off an Arctic iceberg.

"What's your name, Mister?"

"Robert Pettigrew. Big Bob."

Pettigrew had a belly to match his nickname.

"Well, Mister Pettigrew, it seems I'm gonna have to arrest you for destruction of government property and littering."

"What government property? And what in the hell is littering?"

"The poster you just tore up. Littering is tossing trash in the street."

Several more men spilled from the saloon, as well as more from other buildings. They sensed trouble like a dachshund smelled a rat.

"I've got my two men here who say you ain't arresting me or nobody else."

"Is that right?"

"That's right," the man to Pettigrew's left said. "Get out of our way, boss. This won't take long."

Pettigrew edged back through the batwings of his saloon.

"You gonna try to gun me down?"

"Not try. We're damn sure gonna do just that, Marshal."

"Then what are you waiting for?"

Both men grabbed for their guns. Vic drew his

Smith and Wesson in a cross draw so smooth and fast it was merely a blur. He shot the man on the left in his gut before he even cleared leather, shifted his gun and shot the man on the right in the chest, just as he got his gun level. He put a second slug into that man, then shifted his gun again and shot the first man in the gut once more. Both gunfighters staggered and fell, the gut-shot man to his face, the other on his back.

"Ya . . . Ya got us . . . both, Marshal. Damn."

Those were the last words the gut-shot man said. The other one was already dead. He'd never uttered a sound throughout the entire confrontation.

"You killed my employees," Pettigrew screamed, coming through the batwings holding a sawed-off Greener. "Now it's your turn."

Vic turned and put the remaining bullet in his gun into Pettigrew's huge belly. The saloonkeeper seemed to turn to jelly. His fingers triggered both barrels of the shotgun, which discharged its load harmlessly to the dirt. He sagged against the wall, sliding down it to a seated position. His body quivered in its death throes, blood turning his white shirt crimson.

"Anyone else want to try for a piece of me?" Vic demanded, as he punched the empties from his pistol and reloaded, this time filling all six chambers, including the one under the hammer.

"No? Y'all just made a right smart decision.

Big Bob's is officially shut down. Find whoever handles the bodies in this town and get them out of here. Before I have to arrest myself for leaving trash in the street. *Pronto*!"

Vic deliberately turned his back on the spectators. Now was not the time to show fear. He picked up the remaining handbills, crossed the street to Josie's Club, and tacked a handbill alongside the door.

I think I made a good first impression. Now to see what happens.

11

Vic's first order of business the next day was to locate a building which could serve as his office and, with any luck, a jail. The first two he looked at the owners turned him down flat.

The next building he went to was a vacant warehouse with a small office. It was owned by Bertram Hawks Foster, the same man who owned the hardware store. Foster met Vic there.

"I don't know if this is a good idea or not, Marshal, me possibly renting you my warehouse. But it's not doing anything but costing me money sitting empty. Let's go inside so you can look around."

Foster unlocked the door and led Vic inside. He lit a coal oil lamp on the desk and picked it up.

"As you can see, Marshal, the warehouse is divided up into a number of storage rooms. The walls are solid oak, the doors the same. The hinges and locks are all heavy duty, and doubled. I was hoping a freight outfit would start running to Fort Griffin and need a depot. That never happened. No freighter was willing to come into a town as rough as this one. So this building's sat empty from day one. Those storage rooms sure aren't escape proof, but they're the closest thing to cells you'll find here."

Vic went through the building, knocking on the walls, checking the locks, the outside access. He was pleased to find the only doors were in the front of the building. It would be a simple matter to board up the freight door. A few modest changes would turn the warehouse into a fairly secure jail.

"I think I can make this work, Mr. Foster. Let's go back to your store and iron out the details. Will you be able to paint a sign: *UNITED STATES MARSHALS OFFICE AND FORT GRIFFIN JAIL?*"

"Of course. Nothing fancy, I trust."

"Not at all. Black paint, plain font."

"I'll start on it as soon as we sign the contract."

Vic's next stop was the newspaper office. Dale Sullivan was cranking the press, inking the copies of this week's *Echo.*

"Howdy, Dale," Vic shouted to be heard over the noise.

Dale ran one last sheet of paper through the press, then looked up.

"Howdy, Vic. You gave me a damn good headline for the paper this week, killing Big Bob and his men. Looks like you're off to a good start."

"Yup, but it's sure gonna rile up the bad elements in town."

"What brings you by?"

"Two things. I'll be opening an office and jail

in the next few days. They'll be in the Foster Warehouse. I'd like to get that in next week's paper."

"That won't be a problem. What else?"

"I need some more handbills. Seventy of them this time."

"All right. What do they need to say?"

"Let me write it down for you."

With the piece of paper and pencil handed to him, Vic printed out the following:

United States Deputy Marshal Victor Verdugo is Calling a Meeting of all Interested Business Owners to Discuss Matters Concerning the Future of Fort Griffin. Meeting Will Be Held Saturday, June 8 7:00 P.M. at the Beehive Saloon.

"I can get right on those, soon as I finish printing the rest of the papers."

"That's fine. I'll stop by in the morning to pick them up."

"See you then, Vic."

"*Mañana.*"

12

The Butterfield Overland Mail Stage Route ran north and west of Fort Griffin, at the Clear Fork Crossing. Some gut feeling, along with whispered rumors around town, told Vic the stage's next run, two days later, would be intercepted by highwaymen, since it bypassed the town in the middle of the night. The only question was where? The crossing was the most logical point, but with thick brush choking the bottomlands along the river and creeks, any attempt at holding up the stage could be made at almost any point within a twenty-mile stretch. If Vic guessed wrong, the robbers could hit the stage, possibly with loss of innocent lives, then disappear into the tall and uncut, where it would be almost impossible to find them.

Vic had moved into his office, which he'd furnished with a cot he bought at the general store, along with a file cabinet. Foster had included the other furnishings already in the building with the rent. There was a small corral and lean-to out back to shelter Topper, hold his feed and Vic's gear.

Vic made an early afternoon round of Fort Griffin, then returned to the office to cook an early supper, then take a short nap. At dusk, he awoke, saddled and bridled Topper, then rode toward Clear Fork Crossing. Dust hung in the air, indicating the presence of several riders ahead of him.

"Those could just be some travelers headed elsewhere, Topper, but I doubt it," he told his horse, with a pat to his right shoulder. "It's too dangerous in these parts for honest folks to take to the road at night. I'd bet my hat my hunch is right, and the men ahead of us are fixing to hold up the stage. Let's move quiet, now."

Vic kept well back, making certain he could not be seen or heard, nor the riders' horses able to catch Topper's scent. After a while, he could hear them splash across the river, then stop.

"It seems as if I was right about where they've set up their ambush, horse. Let's go downstream a ways then circle back behind them."

Moving as quietly as possible, Vic worked his way to the shelter of a thick clump of redberry junipers. He could see four men concentrating on the crossing, while he was well hidden, They were so intent on watching for the stage to approach it was unlikely any of them would turn to look in his direction anyway.

An hour later, the hoofbeats of six hard-driven horses and the rattling of the Butterfield coach broke the stillness of the night. The four highwaymen rode into the middle of the river. Vic lifted his Winchester from its scabbard, and rode as near as he dared.

The stage came into view. One of the would-be holdup men fired a warning shot into the air. The driver hauled back on the reins, causing the front horses to rear. The shotgun guard grabbed his weapon.

"I wouldn't do that if I were you," one man warned him. The guard let the shotgun drop to his feet.

"Do everything we say and no one'll get hurt," the gang leader ordered.

"No. Do everything *I* say and none of *you* will get hurt," Vic roared. "United States Deputy Marshal. Y'all are under arrest."

Startled, every man turned to look at Vic. One started to fire his gun. Vic knocked him off his horse with a bullet in the chest. He landed in the river with a splash. The other three men also began firing. Vic shot one through the stomach.

The guard had snatched up his shotgun and let loose with both barrels. The spreading buckshot tore into the two remaining men's backs. They slumped over their horses' necks, then slid into the water.

"You all right, Marshal?" the guard called.

"Yeah. How about you fellers?"

"We're fine, thanks to you."

"Good. Let's round up the bodies, load them on their horses, and get them back to town. You'll have to come along so I can get your information for my report."

“Since you saved our hides, we’ll be more than happy to do that,” the driver answered.

The robbers’ horses were gathered, the men’s bodies dragged from the river and tied belly down over their saddles.

When Vic rode into town, leading the horses carrying the dead men, with the Butterfield coach following, it created quite a stir among the denizens of the night. Men pointed and muttered among themselves, ladies of the evening covered their mouths and fanned themselves. Vic stopped at Foster’s Hardware, which doubled as the town’s mortuary, to drop off the bodies. He had two men take the dead men’s horses to the Occidental Hotel’s livery stable. They would be auctioned off to pay for the board and Foster’s charges for the coffins and burying.

After following Vic to his office, where he took statements from the driver, guard, and the two passengers, the stage left Fort Griffin, now two hours behind schedule.

Vic gave Topper a quick rubdown, hay and water, then turned in himself. His report could be finished after he got some much-needed sleep.

13

By seven o'clock Saturday evening, the Beehive Saloon was packed to overflowing. Men stood on the street in front of the place, those who could get close enough peering through its windows.

Vic was using the bar as a makeshift podium. He had invited Colonel Elliott, and was surprised to see the fort's commanding officer actually show up. He gave the colonel a seat at a front table, along with Dale Sullivan from the *Echo*, Doctor Phineas Taylor, who had been cashiered out of the Army, but, realizing a medical practice in Fort Griffin would prove quite lucrative, set up a private practice, and Honey Bee, the woman who owned the Beehive.

At ten minutes past seven, Vic rapped the butt of his pistol on the bar to call the room to order. It took a few minutes before everyone settled down and he was able to speak.

"Good evening. For those of you I might not have yet met, I am United States Deputy Marshal Victor Verdugo. I have been assigned by Chief Federal Justice for the State of Texas, The Honorable Isaiah Canton, to put a stop to the rampant crime in Fort Griffin. I'd like to thank everyone for coming tonight. I intend to keep this meeting as brief as possible.

"I know rumors have been circulating that I intend to shut down most of the "entertainment" businesses in Fort Griffin. That is absolutely untrue. I wish to see every business in this town be successful. However, the present conditions in Fort Griffin make that impossible.

"My objective is to minimize, as much as possible, the numerous robberies, assaults, shootings, stabbings, and killings in this town and the surrounding area. I am not so naïve as to believe I can completely eradicate criminal activities here. That is an impossible task, even in the quietest of cities, with the most professional and efficient police departments. I hardly need tell you that does not describe Fort Griffin, not by the longest stretch of the imagination.

"As most of you are aware, Colonel Elliott has put in a request to the Federal Authorities to declare martial law, and have the Army placed in charge of law enforcement here. That request has been put in abeyance, and will be denied if I am successful in bringing crime in Fort Griffin down to an acceptable level, and a local marshal and deputy appointed.

"I am certain no one, not even the worst outlaw, wants to see any part of Texas placed under Reconstruction law again. If I can get cooperation from most of the citizens and business owners, that need not happen.

"To put to rest some other rumors, I will not

be confiscating anyone's guns or knives. There will be no law established, as in many other cities, requiring guns be checked with the local authorities, in this case me, and returned upon leaving town. That said, the shooting of any firearm, of any type, within the city limits will be banned. Anyone who fires a weapon will be subject to arrest, the weapon confiscated. It will not be returned, but either sold at auction or destroyed. Let me finish speaking," Vic said, when a wave of objections swept through the room.

"Another rumor is soldiers from the fort, in particular buffalo soldiers, will no longer be permitted to patronize businesses in Fort Griffin. That is also not true. Those establishments which welcome Negroes will be allowed to continue to serve their clientele. Any white person who interferes with a Negro's right to walk the streets of this city, shop at the stores or have a meal or drink at the places which cater to them, will be charged with disorderly conduct. Or more serious charges, depending on the severity of the infraction. That permission, of course, is subject to being modified or overruled by Colonel Elliott, the fort's commanding officer.

"That's the basics. I'm not much for talking, and I've said my piece. I will take a few questions. Please state your name and position when called upon."

Vic indicated a man in the back.

"You, sir."

"Charles Montgomery, owner of the Lady Gay Saloon. Do you intend to arrest men for public drunkenness?"

"Yes. If that is their only violation, they will be jailed overnight, then turned loose in the morning. Next. The lady in the fourth row."

"Madge Lowry, owner of Madge's Home for Wayward Girls. Will you be shutting down my type of business?"

"Only if it becomes a public nuisance. That means it will behoove you to keep your clients peaceable. And your "wayward girls" from becoming too forward. Next. You, right in front of me, sir."

"Dalton Mabry, owner of the Palace Gambling Hall. We've all seen how you handled the issue with Bob Pettigrew."

"That was unfortunate. If Mr. Pettigrew hadn't accosted me, and sicced two of his gun slicks on me, he and both those men would still be alive. In fact, Mr. Pettigrew *would* still be alive, had he not turned his shotgun on me.

"Let me make one thing perfectly clear. Fort Griffin has a reputation as one of the wickedest, most dangerous, most lawless cities in not just Texas, but the entire West. That has to change if the town is to survive. I intend to make that happen."

Mabry spoke again.

"You have earned the sobriquet *The Executioner.* Do you intend to embellish your reputation off the backs and dead bodies of the citizens of Fort Griffin?"

"That is an unfortunate title which I neither wanted, nor sought. It came about because the English translation of my surname is Executioner. In my line of work it is sometimes necessary to kill a person to stop their crimes, or save innocent lives. I do not enjoy killing anyone, but I will never hesitate to kill those who endanger the public. I'm calling this meeting to a close. If anyone has further questions, you know where my office is located. I'll be there to meet with anyone who so desires Monday through Saturday, from nine to eleven in the morning. Good night, and by working together, we can make Fort Griffin a city to be proud of."

14

The next morning, Vic was having coffee with Dale Sullivan in the office of the *Fort Griffin Echo.*

"Boy howdy, Vic, that little scolding you gave the town last night is really gonna stir things up around here," Dale said. "Most folks in this place prefer to keep it just the way it is."

"Dale, it doesn't matter what they want. The town can't stay the way it is. If I can't calm it down, the Army will. And when the Army closes the fort and pulls out . . ."

"You mean if."

"I mean when. Look, most of the Indian tribes have already been subjugated and forced onto reservations. You don't have to like it, or agree with the government's policy, I surely don't, of forcing people off the lands they've roamed for thousands of years, but that's the way it's always been, throughout the course of human history, going all the way back to Alexander the Great and even earlier. Egyptians enslave Hebrews, Mongols sweep through Asia, Rome conquers everyone, then the Vandals push the Romans out. And on and on and on. It'll still be that way long after you and I are gone. So once the last of the renegade Indian bands are killed off and the few survivors forced onto the reservations with the others, there will no longer be any need for a string of forts to protect the frontier. If Fort Griffin, or any other towns dependent on the Army for their existence don't plan ahead and adapt for the future, they'll dry up and blow away. Especially those bypassed by the railroads. And I'm willing to bet Fort Griffin is one of those. No railroad, no reason for the town to exist. People will just move on to better pickings. There'll be nothing left here but a few tumbledown ruins and some cellar holes."

"You sure are a cheery cuss, Marshal Verdugo."

"Not cheery. Just realistic, and a student of history. Most great civilizations or empires last on average about two hundred and fifty years. Someday the United States of America won't exist, or exist only as a no longer influential, minor country, living on its past glory."

"You do realize you might have bitten off way more than you can chew?"

"Did it occur to you that you might have done the same, Dale? Your editorials about the conditions in Fort Griffin and the need for law and order to take the place of the present system, which is well-nigh anarchy, are not being taken well by some of the worst actors in these parts. I hope you know enough to watch your back."

"I wear my six-gun at all times, and sleep with it alongside me," Dale answered. "The day the press becomes too afraid to speak up against injustices, corruption, or crime is the day America starts to lose its hard-fought for freedoms."

"It's a damn shame more people don't think like you."

The newspaper's door slammed open. A young boy of about eleven came rushing in, out of breath.

"Marshal . . . Marshal. Glad I found you."

"Take it easy son. Catch your breath. What's your name?"

"Joey. Joey Hallston. There's two dead men. Behind the Cavalry House Saloon."

"Dale, isn't that one of the places the buffalo soldiers frequent?"

"It sure is, Marshal."

"Let's go. Joey, lead the way."

Vic grabbed his hat from Dale's desk and jammed it on his head. He, Dale, and Joey headed out the door on the run. Vic mounted Topper and followed the boy, with Dale right alongside.

The Cavalry House was at the southwest end of town, nearest the fort itself. This section was where most of the businesses which catered to the buffalo soldiers were located. The saloon was in a hastily thrown together structure of raw, unpainted lumber. A small crowd was gathered out front.

"Clear the way!" Vic ordered, as he jumped off his horse. "Let me through."

The crowd split as if Moses had just parted the Red Sea.

"Where's the dead men, Joey?"

"Straight out back. I found them, lyin' there all bloody, the flies and rats feeding on them. Made me real queasy."

Vic pointed to two of the spectators.

"You, go find Doc Taylor. You, round up this place's owner."

"I'm right here, Marshal," a man answered, stepping out of the curious bystanders. "Kiowa Parks. Joey found the men when he was helping me clean up."

Parks was a half-breed, with the dark hair and high cheekbones of a Kiowa, but lighter skinned and gray eyed. He was dressed in buckskins, with moccasins on his feet.

"Then you come with me. You too, Joey, if you can handle it. The rest of you, stay back. Send Doc Taylor to me soon as he gets here."

Two black men, dressed in soldiers' uniforms, lay sprawled in the dirt several yards behind the saloon. One was face down, the other lying on his back. Both had been scalped.

"Damn," Vic cursed. "This is exactly what I didn't want to see. Two dead buffalo soldiers. This could be the spark that turns the entire town into a raging inferno. Mister Parks, send someone to the fort. Let Colonel Elliott know what's happened, and that he'll need a detail with a buckboard to haul these men back there."

"Right away."

While Parks did Vic's bidding, the marshal questioned Joey.

"You didn't touch anything, did you, son?"

Joey shook his head.

"No sir. Mr. Parks didn't either. I work for him, helping him clean up the mess left after a night of a bunch of soldiers drinking, gambling, and whoring."

Vic shook his head in disgust. A lad as young as Joey shouldn't know about such things. It could be a tough life for a youngster, growing up in a Western frontier town.

"You didn't see anyone else?"

"No. I could tell for sure those fellers were both dead, though."

Parks returned.

"There's two men headed up to the fort, Marshal."

Vic rolled the prone man onto his back.

"Good. Do you know either of these men?"

"Only as Hawley and Honesdale. They came in pretty regular. They left last night about an hour before closing. That was one o'clock. They'd get a little too drunk every so often, but they weren't really troublemakers."

"Did anyone leave with them?"

"Nope."

"Who was still here when you closed up for the night?"

"Just me. It was a slow night, so I sent Chuck Riggs, my other bartender, home early."

"Who were the last ones to leave?"

"Let me think. A couple of other soldiers. Oh yeah. Four buffalo hunters. Must've been new to these parts, leastwise I'd never seen them before. Usual type, dirty, greasy, smelly. One stood out, though. He had skin so pale it was almost fish belly white. Hair the same, blonde but looked almost pure white. Pale blue eyes. If a person ran into him at night they'd have sworn they'd come across a ghost."

"Let me take a closer look at these bodies. You just might've given me a good clue as to whom I'll be searching for, Mr. Parks."

"That one's Hawley, Marshal," Parks said, as Vic hunkered alongside one of the bodies.

"He was lyin' face down. I rolled him onto his back. He was stabbed a number of times in his lower back, and his throat was slit wide open. He and his friend must've been taken by surprise. You didn't hear any sign of a struggle?"

"Not a sound. Of course, my hearing ain't what it used to be. But if there'd been a fight, I'd have heard it."

"This other one, Honesdale. He took a knife to the stomach, and it was ripped wide open. Kind of unusual he didn't scream from the pain. I reckon one of the killers grabbed him from behind, kept his mouth covered, while one of the others gutted him. The wounds were made by a heavy bladed knife. The killers knew exactly what they were doing. Everything points to those hide hunters. Let me check their pockets."

Vic went through the dead men's clothing, finding they had been stripped clean of anything valuable.

"This was a murder-robbery, all right," he said. "There's tracks headed off toward the Brazos. They shouldn't be too hard to follow. As soon as the soldiers from the fort get here, I'll start trailing those *hombres*."

"You're gonna wait?" Parks questioned. "The sons of bitches have already got a good head start."

"I know, but I'd imagine Colonel Elliott will want at least one of his men with me. I'm not worried about the bastards having a lead. They probably have a camp somewhere in the river bottoms. They were no doubt liquored up, so they'll have had to stop and sleep it off. They also most likely figure no one would worry too much about a couple of buffalo soldiers. They're about to find out how wrong they are."

Vic rolled and lit a cigarette while he continued searching for clues. It was a little less than half an hour later when Colonel Elliott arrived, accompanied by two other men. He nodded curtly at Vic.

"Marshal. What have you got here?"

"Two of your men, names of Hawley and Honesdale, according to Mr. Parks. They've been stabbed and scalped. Mr. Parks has given me a good idea of who the killers are. Four hide hunters. They left a real clear trail. I'm about to go after them, but I waited for you. I'm certain you'll want to send one of your men along to assist me."

"You're damn right I do. This here is Sergeant Finnegan O'Toole. With him is Tonkawa scout Charley Two Feathers. They're the best man-hunters at the fort."

"Then we won't waste any more time. I'm sorry about your men, Colonel. I'll try to bring their killers back alive to face military justice."

"That's a bit out of order, isn't it, Marshal?"

"It is. However, since the victims were cavalrymen with the United States Army, there's no nearby civilian court, and with Reconstruction not completely ended, in this case a military trial is appropriate. Plus I'd imagine you'll want the satisfaction of meting out justice."

"You imagine right, Marshal. Finnegan, Charley, do everything necessary to avenge the foul murders of your comrades."

"Yes sir, Colonel."

O'Toole gave Elliott a salute, while Two Feathers simply nodded.

Vic mounted up.

"Let's get those skunks."

15

"Those men appear to be making a beeline straight northwest, Marshal," O'Toole said, after they'd followed the tracks of four horses for two miles.

"To white men, that would make sense," Two Feathers said. "They would want to get to the river bottoms as fast as possible. They would believe they were safe once they got into the tangled brush, thick trees, and soft ground. The river also bends back on itself quite a lot north of here, so it would afford plenty of places for those men to double back, cross the river many times. That would confuse any pursuit. However, Indians know to blot out as much of a trail as possible as you go along. Not hiding their tracks, as the men we are following are doing, makes it much easier to find wherever they stop, or to catch up with them, since we won't lose the trail and have to waste time picking it up again."

"How far ahead of us do you think they are, Charley?"

"I'm not certain, Marshal. Two hours at most. We should run them down before nightfall."

"That's good, because we wouldn't want to ride right up to their camp without knowing it," Vic said.

"Shure and begorrrah, I'm worried about them realizing they're being followed, and setting up an ambush for us," O'Toole said. "You know what a Sharps Big Fifty can do to a man. Blow a hole the size of a fist clean through him at five hundred yards."

"They don't seem that smart," Vic said.

"I hope you're right, Marshal," O'Toole replied.

"With all due respect, Marshal, if you'll allow me to take the lead we'll have less trouble running those men to ground," Two Feathers said. "The sergeant is an excellent tracker, as I imagine are you. However, very few white men can track as well as an Indian. That's why the Texas Rangers found Tonkawa scouts so valuable. Of course then the state turned around and forced us onto reservations, that's the thanks we got. But being bitter won't help my people survive."

"You go right ahead, Charley. This isn't about who can do what better. It's about bringing four cold-blooded murderers in to face justice, and pay for their crimes."

They were nearing the Clear Fork when Two Feathers raised his hand, telling the others to stop as he pulled his pinto to a halt.

"We are very close now. The river makes an oxbow bend here. Just upriver is a buffalo wallow, which makes for easy hunting. People of all races and tribes have been camping here since the Great Spirit first brought life to the earth. I can also scent wood smoke on the air. We go on foot from here. If either of your horses might call out, tie a bandanna around his muzzle. They will be content to stay here and graze while we go after our quarry. Remove your spurs and anything else which might make noise and give us away. I would advise leaving your rifles. It would be too easy for them to snag on a branch and snap it with a loud crack. I'll get us in close enough so that pistols will be sufficient."

They dismounted, tying their horses loosely so they could easily pick at the grass or tender leaves of salt cedar and scrub willow.

"You keep quiet now, Horatio, me bonnie lad," O'Toole ordered his horse. "You know what to do."

After divesting themselves of spurs, extra shells, anything metallic that might clink, making a sound that would seem as loud as a Rebel yell in the brush, the three men moved forward.

"There's no possible way we can capture all of them," Two Feathers said. "The terrain and the river make it impossible to surround them. Surprise is our only hope. And the sudden death of at least one is how we make that happen."

They worked their way through the brush, dropping low here to avoid an overhanging branch, circling around clumps of cactus there, stepping over narrow creeks and muddy bogs which could suck a man's boots off.

Two Feathers held up his hand.

"Wait."

The laughter of men could be heard. Three could also be seen, through a thin screen of vegetation.

"I'll take one. What about the others, Marshal?"

"We give them one chance to surrender. If they put up a fight, or try to run, we shoot to kill."

"Time to make our move."

Two Feathers took an arrow from the quiver hung over his shoulder, notched it to his bow. He went low, stopping just before he would break into the clearing.

He took careful aim and let the arrow fly. It thudded into the belly of the pale eyed hide hunter. The man screeched in pain and terror, his eyes wide with shock. He grasped the arrow's shaft and tugged at it, trying futilely to yank it out of his gut. Two Feathers put another arrow into him, just alongside the first. The man went down hard.

The other men jumped to their feet, confused, looking around desperately for the source of the arrow.

Vic's voice boomed as thunder rumbling.

"United States Deputy Marshal! You're all under arrest. Throw down your weapons and get your hands in the air. Try to run and we'll cut you down where you stand."

The three men still on their feet ignored Vic's

order. They grabbed for their guns. Two went down with bullets in their chests. The third caught an arrow from Two Feathers in his right thigh. He toppled to his side, writhing in pain.

Guns still at the ready, the lawman, soldier, and Tonkawa scout emerged into the clearing. Two of the hide hunters were already dead. O'Toole went up to an injured one, kicked his gun out of reach, and stuck his gun against the man's nose.

"By me sainted mother, if you so much as wiggle I'll blow your brains out. Those men you bastards killed were two of the bravest soldiers to ever serve in the United States Cavalry."

"I've got him, Sergeant," Vic said. He rolled the man onto his side and handcuffed him behind his back.

"We'll make certain you live long enough to get back to Fort Griffin and face a firing squad."

There was no response. The hide hunter had passed out.

A high-pitched scream tore through the air. Charley Two Feathers held a bloody blonde scalp high over his head, whooping in triumph. He'd taken his prize just before his quarry died. Two Feathers next went to the other dead men, and took their scalps.

"Three scalps, including a yellow hair, a prize to make any warrior a hero," he said, grinning. "Today was a good day for the Tonkawa people."

"Their horses and wagon are just beyond those

trees," Vic said. "Let's load them up. We can be back to the fort before dark."

It was late in the afternoon when Vic and his companions arrived back at Fort Griffin.

"I see you caught up with those men," Colonel Elliott said, as he met them. "Good work. Sergeant O'Toole, Scout Two Feathers, you'll both receive commendations for this."

"Thank you, Colonel," Two Feathers said.

"Yes sir. Thank you indeed," O'Toole answered.

"I'm sorry we couldn't bring them all back alive for you, Colonel," Vic said. "But they put up a fight. You still have one for the stockade, though. And your men did an excellent job making certain we found them, and that they were unable to escape."

"As long as these scum have been removed from the Earth, it's all that matters, Marshal. I thank you for your efforts. I, and the men of Fort Griffin, are most grateful."

"Thank you for that, Colonel. Now, unless you need me for something, I'm going to take care of Topper, clean up, grab some chow, then turn in. I'll write up my report and have a copy to you in the morning."

"That is perfectly all right. Get a good night's rest. You deserve it."

"Then I'll say good night, Colonel."

"Good night, Marshal."

16

Two days later, Vic was in his office when a hard-bitten looking man walked in.

"Howdy. You the Marshal?"

"I am. United States Deputy Marshal Victor Verdugo. What can I do for you?"

"Lance Pollard. Trail boss for the SA Cross Ranch south of San Antonio."

Pollard was a big man, nearly six feet tall and around two hundred pounds. His sun bronzed and wrinkled skin made it hard to determine his age. Vic would estimate somewhere in his mid-thirties. He had dark brown hair and eyes, was dressed in dust-covered range clothing. His manner was brusque.

"I see. I take it you've got a herd coming up the Great Western Trail?"

"Purty near two thousand head of prime beef on the hoof, on the way to Dodge City. We bedded down a day's distance south of here last night, then started moving again at first light. We're gonna spend tonight just outside of town here, then move on first thing tomorrow."

"I appreciate your courtesy of giving me notice, Mr. Pollard."

"I figured I should. The boys are gonna want to blow off some steam. I expect you know what that means."

"If you mean shooting up the town, getting into fights, and destruction of property, I do. So get this straight. None of that's going to happen. Your men are more than welcome to come into town, get a good meal, drink, gamble, and dally with some of our female entertainers. However, any one of 'em who starts the least bit of trouble will be tossed in a cell. He'll have to pay a fine before he's turned loose. Any real problem like shooting or assault will land that man in jail, and he'll stay there until the circuit judge arrives. And since there's no circuit courts established here yet, that means whenever one has the time to head up this way. The bottom line is keep your hands under control, or you'll be leaving Fort Griffin with fewer than you arrived with."

"You can't issue orders like that. Besides, Fort Griffin is a wide-open town."

"I can, and I just did. Things are changing here, Mr. Pollard. I was ordered to Fort Griffin to tame this town. I'm doing just that."

"We'll see about that tonight," Pollard said.

"Don't threaten me, Mister. Or I'll throw your damn butt in a cell right now. Oh, and in case you get the brilliant idea to run your cows through town, there will be a line of men armed with shotguns and rifles just waiting for you. They'll down the leaders, the ones behind those will start falling over them, more will pile up and start trampling each other, and by the time you can round up what's left you'll be lucky to find five hundred head. And far fewer cowboys to handle them, because a lot of your men will die too. You can bet your hat on that."

"We'll see."

"The responsibility is yours. Either make certain your men come into town, have some fun, then leave without any problems, or turn them loose and prepare for a battle, the likes of which you've never seen."

"Wait a minute. Marshal Verdugo. You're The Executioner."

"That's right," Vic confirmed. An evil grin spread across his face. "So you know who you're up against."

Pollard turned and walked out of the office, slamming the door behind him.

Vic leaned back in his chair and sighed. How he hated that nickname he'd been hung with. However, at times like this, he did have to admit it came in handy.

"Time to get ready for tonight."

17

As he'd expected, Vic found few takers when he offered to swear in anyone as special deputies to help patrol Fort Griffin that night. Joey Hallston offered, but he was far too young for the job. Vic did allow him to stay in the livery stable's hay loft, to act as a lookout and give warning when men rode into town. Emanuel Perez, one of the guards at the Honey Bee Saloon, signed on at the urging of his boss. She ran a quiet, respectable place, at least by Fort Griffin standards, and she intended to keep it that way. Jules Yankton and Hank Zee, who together owned the town's saddle and harness shop, also signed on, as did Dale Sullivan, the newspaperman. Five men, only one of whom was an experienced lawman, to take on who knew how many drunken cowpunchers and horse wranglers.

"We'll stay in pairs," he told the new deputies. "Until there's trouble. Emanuel, you'll be with me; Jules, you and Hank work together, so you'll work as a team. Dale, you stay at your office. It's centrally located, so you can go from there in any direction you're needed. With any luck, we'll only have to crack a few heads tonight. With a whole lot of luck, maybe not even that."

"Begging your pardon, Marshal, but you're a

helluva lot more optimistic than I am," Perez said.

"It's just wishful thinking," Vic answered. "I'm hoping against hope there won't be any bloodshed tonight. Let me hand out your weapons."

Earlier that afternoon, Vic had visited Staley's Gun Shop, where he purchased five brand new Remington shotguns, along with fifteen boxes of shells. He handed one gun and three boxes of shells to each man, who already had their personal revolvers in gun belts strapped around their waists. He had also gone to Foster's Hardware to buy a key to the jail for each man.

"We'll walk around town, stopping in at the usual trouble spots, the saloons, gambling dens, and brothels. If anyone looks like he's about to start trouble, send him on his way out of town. If he refuses, toss him in a cell. Knock him over the head if you have to. We're not playing games here. At the least sign your lives, or the lives of innocent folks, are in danger from anyone, use those shotguns. One warning shot, then if they keep comin' let them have it. Seeing four or five men cut down by buckshot stops most mobs in their tracks. And of course since the rest of us will hear the gunfire we'll come a-runnin' to lend a hand. Let's get some supper. The Marshals Service will pick up the tab."

The SA Cross herd gave away its presence long before it reached the night's bedding ground.

The bawling of cattle, the shouting of cowboys, whinnying of horses, thunder of thousands of hooves, and the massive dust cloud thrown up by the river of beef rose over the noise of Fort Griffin's streets.

Vic had caught one break. Colonel Elliott had agreed to keep his men confined to their quarters that night, which meant one less matchstick to light the powder keg that was Fort Griffin. Texans had no love for Federal troops, and most of the troops, who were from the North, felt the same way about the Texans they were supposed to protect from Indian depredations. Since most of the enlisted men at Fort Griffin were blacks, buffalo soldiers, they were despised by many of the southerners who still smarted over losing the war, and who still believed blacks should be kept enslaved. Out here in west Texas, the racial difference didn't matter quite so much, since slavery had never been a viable option for running ranches, unlike the cotton plantations in east Texas. In addition, many of the freed slaves had drifted west and hired on as cooks, cowhands and horse wranglers. Some crews consisted of as much as forty percent blacks and Hispanics. But racial animosity still bubbled just underneath the surface in much of the former Confederacy. Far better to keep the soldiers of Fort Griffin confined for one night than to chance an all-out riot.

Stragglers began drifting into town around eight o'clock. There were cowboys and homesteaders from the region, along with people travelling through to places farther west. They went into the various restaurants, cafes, saloons, gambling parlors and sporting houses for meals and an evening's entertainment.

At twenty to nine, Joey gave three shrill whistles from the livery stable. He pointed to the south end of town, where at least forty riders were approaching *en masse.* Lance Pollard was in the lead, with a vicious looking Mexican on a prancing white gelding alongside him.

Vic acknowledged Joey's warning, then he and Perez walked slowly done the middle of the street, advancing until they were about fifty feet from the SA Cross crew. They held their shotguns ready to bring level and fire at a moment's notice.

"Hold it right there," Vic ordered.

"Evenin', Marshal," Pollard said.

"Evenin' yourself, Mr. Pollard. I trust you didn't have any trouble moving your herd today."

"No, we didn't. Some of the boys are watching the cows. The rest have come into town to work off some excess energy and have a good time. It's a long way to the next town, so I promised them a night here in Fort Griffin."

"I'm certain they deserve it. As you and I discussed, they can have all the fun they want, as long as it doesn't involve shootings, thefts, fights, or destruction of property. There are a good number of establishments here which cater to the cattlemen, soldiers, and buffalo hunters who pass through town. We want y'all to have a good time. However, if any trouble starts, we are prepared to handle it."

"We make our own kind of *divertido*, *gringo*," the Mexican said, sneering. No *Yanqui* tells us what we can or can't do. Particularly I, Jose Montalvo."

"Suit yourself," Vic said, with a shrug. "Mr. Pollard, you might want to explain to your *niño pequeño* how a bellyful of buckshot is a horrible way to die."

At that insult, Montalvo started for his pistol.

"Hold it right there, Jose," Pollard ordered. "We'll abide by the marshal's rules. There's always another town where the folks aren't so fussy about their customers acting like church ladies."

"You're showing good sense, Mr. Pollard," Vic said. "I just want to add one thing. If anyone who is not one of your hands starts trouble, don't try to handle it yourself. Find me or one of my deputies. The law in Fort Griffin applies to visitors and residents alike."

"What if someone pulls a gun on one of my men?"

"As long as your man fires in justifiable self-defense, he will have a hearing tonight, and if innocent he will be free to go."

"That sounds fair enough. I'll do my best to keep the boys in check, Marshal. Men, let's go."

Vic and Perez stepped aside to let the SA Cross riders pass. They turned in at various saloons, tied their horses, and went inside, whooping and hollering.

"Do you really think Pollard will be able to control that bunch, Vic?"

"*Quien sabe*, Emanuel. But I'm hoping and praying to God he will. Otherwise, it's going to be an awful bloody night."

The night passed more quietly than Vic had dared hope. Only four men were in the jail, three of them from the SA Cross, one a townsman. They had all been charged with public intoxication, and would be turned loose the next morning.

Things were winding down, most of the men headed back to their spreads or homesteads, many of the SA Cross riders had already gone back to where the herd was bedded down, bringing bottles of whiskey for those who had remained behind to guard the herd.

Vic and Perez were walking past the Honey Bee Saloon when two men stumbled out, Jose Montalvo and another cowboy, who was short and stout, with shoulder length light brown hair and muddy brown eyes. They stopped short when they saw the marshal and deputy.

"*Mariscal*!" Montalvo shouted. "No one insults me as you did and lives to tell about it. You are about to find that out."

"You're drunk, Montalvo. Go back to your herd and sleep it off."

"Never! I am going to take you apart with my bare hands."

Montalvo unbuckled his gun belt and tossed it aside. Vic did the same.

"We've had a quiet night, Montalvo. Why start trouble now?"

"Because I will not be insulted by a damn *Yanqui*!"

Montalvo rushed at Vic, who easily sidestepped the move. Both men circled each other now, looking for an opening. Vic shot a quick right at Montalvo's jaw. Montalvo ducked it and sent a hard left into Vic's right ribs. He followed that with a jolting right low into Vic's gut. Vic jackknifed, fell to his side, and rolled away from Montalvo's attempted kick to his groin. He grabbed Montalvo's right ankle, twisted hard. With a screech, Montalvo fell to the ground. He and Vic rolled over and over, each grappling to get a grip on his opponent.

Montalvo got to his feet first. He pulled a heavy bladed knife from the sheath on his left hip. He waited until Vic got up, then lunged at him.

The knife tore a slice along Vic's left side.

Vic pulled out his own knife. He feinted a move to Montalvo's belly, then when the Mexican twisted aside, slashed at his right wrist. Vic's sharp blade completely separated Montalvo's hand from his arm. It fell to the road, still gripping the knife. Montalvo sat down hard on the boardwalk in front of the Honey Bee, crying, blood spurting from the stump of his arm.

"Emanuel, go find Doc Taylor," Vic ordered.

"On my way."

"You," he told the other cowboy. "Do you want any part of this?"

"No sir, Marshal. I tried to stop that damn fool, but he wouldn't listen."

"Smart choice. Take off your neckerchief. I need it to make a tourniquet to try and keep your pardner from bleeding out before the doc can get here. Also your gun so I can tighten it."

The cowboy untied his neckerchief and handed it to Vic, along with his six-gun. Vic had Montalvo lie down, then held his arm up to keep it above heart level. He wrapped the neckerchief around Montalvo's arm, knotted it around the six-gun's barrel, and twisted it tight. The flow of blood immediately slowed to merely a trickle.

"I sure hope Emanuel doesn't have too much trouble finding the doc," Vic muttered.

A small crowd gathered. One of them was Dale

Sullivan, who had heard the commotion, and raced over to see if he could help.

"The rest of the town's quiet, Vic. What happened here?"

"This damn fool was all liquored up. Said he was gonna kill me."

"I see it didn't work."

Vic loosened the tourniquet slightly.

"No, but if the doc doesn't get here soon, he'll bleed out."

"Maybe this will help?"

Sullivan picked up a bloody object from the dirt.

"Here. Let me give you a hand."

Sullivan began laughing.

Vic looked at him in disbelief.

"You are one damn sick individual, Sullivan."

"At least I didn't put my foot in my mouth. Here comes Doc Taylor."

"What have you got here, Marshal?"

"An amputated hand. I've kept the bleeding to a minimum."

"I see. Good work. Bring this man to my office and I'll get to work. I believe I will be able to save him. What about you, Marshal? You seem to have been wounded."

"It's not deep. I can fix myself up easily enough."

Jules Yankton and Hank Zee walked up. Between them was Lance Pollard.

"Marshal! What the hell happened here? I thought my men were on real good behavior tonight."

"They were, for the most part. Unfortunately, your *segundo* here figured to beat me to death. When that didn't work, he tried his damndest to gut me. I had to defend myself."

"Is that right, Tony?" Pollard asked the other SA Cross hand.

"It is," Tony confirmed. "Jose saw the marshal from inside the saloon. He about went berserk. I tried to talk him out of making a damn fool of himself, but he shoved me aside and ran out the door. The marshal did his best to avoid a fight, but Jose was crazy drunk. You know what he's like when he's had too much to drink."

"If you're his boss, and you'll help me get him to my office, I need to operate right away," Taylor said.

"Will he be able to travel, that is, if there aren't any charges against him?" Pollard asked.

"There won't be," Vic said. "Losing a hand is punishment enough."

"He will, but you'll have to be very careful to change the dressings and keep the wound clean," Taylor said. "The chance of infection is high."

"Our cook was a surgeon's assistant with the Texas Tenth Infantry during the war. He'll know what needs to be done."

"Then I'll release this man to you in the morning."

"Hank, you and Jules should be able to handle the town for the rest of the night," Vic said. "Kind of ease people on home. I'm going to my office, clean up, take care of this wound and get some sleep. Come get me if you need me."

"What about me?" Sullivan asked.

"You can also work for the rest of the night, but I figure you'd rather be writing up a story for this week's paper," Vic answered.

"You're right. G'night, Marshal."

"G'night, all of you. You did a fine job. And I'm obliged to you also, Mr. Pollard. Except for this one incident, your men handled themselves well. The SA Cross is welcome back in Fort Griffin anytime."

"*Gracias*, Marshal."

Jose Montalvo was taken to Doctor Taylor's office for surgery. The few people still prowling the streets of Fort Griffin soon drifted away.

Vic went back to his office, where he peeled off his shirt to get a better look at the knife gash along his ribs. As he'd expected from the lack of blood, it was indeed shallow. He washed out the wound, then the rest of his upper torso. He dried off, washed out the wound again, sprinkled sulfur powder into it, then placed a bandage over it, tying that in place with a strip of cloth.

He sat on the edge of his bed, took off his

gun belt and placed it on the floor, within easy reach, then pulled off his boots, socks, hat, and bandanna. He stretched out on his back, holding his rosary beads. He said two rosaries in gratitude that the night had passed with no deaths and only one serious injury, then drifted off to sleep.

18

Since Fort Griffin had no Post Office or Western Union, Vic sent and received all his mail and telegrams through the fort. He sent a telegraph to Judge Canton about the incident with the SA Cross drovers, along with a summary of the entire previous month. His full reports were given to the fort's postmaster to be sent to Austin.

Colonel Elliott invited Vic to share a noon day meal with him. Vic readily accepted, since he was tired of his own cooking and restaurant food. Besides, he was supposed to establish and maintain cordial relations with the Army. What better way to do that than by partaking of a meal with Fort Griffin's commanding officer.

The meal was served in an elegantly furnished dining room, quite different from the rest of the fort's crude quarters. The table was set with fine bone china, crystal glasses, and sterling silverware, the table covered with a crisply starched white linen tablecloth, napkins of the same material alongside each place setting. A private in full dress uniform would serve the meal.

"Corporal Willington is an excellent cook, Marshal," Elliott said. "He's been with me for several years now. He's a permanent part of my command. Where I go, he goes. I do like to eat well."

"Corporal Willington?" Vic echoed.

"Yes, Corporal James Willington. Why do you ask?"

"Because if he was Corporal *Wellington* he could serve Beef Wellington."

"Marshal, your sense of humor is drier than the driest white wine I have here in this Godforsaken wilderness."

"You haven't heard anything until you hear Dale Sullivan crack a joke."

"Ah yes. The newspaper editor. I have heard some of his wisecracks. Unfortunately, I must say."

Even though their server was right in the room, Elliott picked up a small silver bell and rang it. The private came to Elliott's right side and snapped to attention.

"Yes sir, Colonel?"

"Private Thompson. You may pour the wine, then bring the first course."

"Yes, sir."

Thompson took a bottle of wine from a sideboard, uncorked it, and poured each man's glass half full.

"This is a very dry German Riesling, Marshal," Elliott said, as he swirled the contents of his glass and sniffed the bouquet. "It will pair very well with the mixed greens salad which is our first course, the *soupe de poulet* which is our second course, and the smoked salmon, our third course. Naturally, we shall have shaved ice between each course to cleanse our palates."

"Naturally," Vic said, somehow managing to keep the sarcasm out of his voice. He well knew the poor, often half-spoiled rations the regular troopers received, the men who did most of the fighting, while the officers took credit for any victories, yet blaming their subordinates for any losses. The reservation Indians were treated even worse, much of the food distributed to them rancid, if it indeed arrived at all, not stolen or diverted by dishonest Indian agents to line their own pockets.

Thompson returned with two plates of salad, placing one in front of Vic, the other in front of Elliott.

"I'd like to propose a toast," Elliott said. "To the days when the West is tamed, and peace reigns over this entire land."

"I can drink to that," Vic said. He and Elliott clinked glasses, and took sips of their wine.

"This is quite good," Vic said.

"I knew you would appreciate it," Elliott answered. "It must be a pleasant change from the swill you get in backwater country saloons."

"It is indeed," Vic agreed. He picked up his fork and took a bite of his salad.

"This is even better, Colonel. It's almost impossible to find fresh vegetables out here on the frontier. Usually it's pinto beans or black-eyed peas. Even most times when you find apple pie, it's made from dried apples, not fresh."

"Yes, that is a shame. Johnny Appleseed did his best to establish apple orchards throughout the country, but he never made it this far west. That probably doesn't matter, however. The climate here is not conducive for apple trees to even survive, let alone thrive."

The meal continued for seven courses, the main one being roast beef, dessert apple tarts, accompanied by brandy, then coffee.

"I really appreciated your hospitality, Colonel, and I'm obliged for the meal. Everything was delicious," Vic said, after taking his last swallow of coffee. "However, I've really got to get back to work. Thank you again for confining your men to the fort. It made things easier for all of us. I'm hopeful that was the last time I'll have to make such a request."

"It was a good reminder for the men they're in the Army, not on some kind of holiday. I've got to send two patrols out tomorrow, so they will be more rested than if some of them received a pass to go into town."

"Indian trouble?"

"We've received reports of a number of ranches northeast of here being raided. The indications are some Kiowas have jumped the reservation. By the time we get to where the raids took place, those renegades will probably already be back in the Territories, and of course no one will know anything about Kiowas or Comanches on the warpath."

"Good luck finding them, Colonel. This was their land long before us whites showed up, and they know it far better than we do."

"Someday they'll realize there are too many of us, and too few of them, Marshal."

"That will be a sad day for all of us. Thank you again, Colonel. Good-bye."

"Good-bye, Marshal."

19

Vic's next stop was at the *Fort Griffin Echo.* Dale Sullivan was hard at work, printing the special edition he'd planned. He looked up when Vic walked in, and the bell attached to the door tinkled.

"I'll be right with you, Vic," he called. "Just have the last copies coming off the press."

"I'm in no hurry," Vic answered. He took a chair and turned it toward the front window, where he could watch the activity on the street.

Sullivan pulled the final sheet of paper off the press and handed it to Vic.

MARSHAL VERDUGO KEEPS PEACE DURING A VOLATILE NIGHT IN FORT GRIFFIN!

Vic winced at the blaring headline.

"Read the entire article, and my editorial. Tell me what you think," Sullivan urged.

Vic read through the front-page story, then the editorial on the reverse of the single sheet paper.

"Well, what do you think?"

"I think you've just stepped on a lot of toes, Dale. I can name at least half a dozen saloon owners who'd like to put you out of business for what you've written. Not to mention several gambling hall and brothel owners."

"I'm not going to pull the paper," Dale said.

"I'm not asking you to. I'm just trying to let you know what you'll be up against."

"I'm well aware of that. Vic, no matter how many lawmen are sent into a town, if the citizens aren't in favor of law and order that town will never settle down. There's talk of opening an academy here in Fort Griffin. And of course the railroads will be building this way. They can easily bypass the town if they think it's more trouble than it's worth. No railroad, no businesses that people need, not just saloons and their like, no schools, no churches, streets not safe for decent citizens to walk, then there's no town."

Joey Hallston came rushing into the office.

"Howdy, Marshal. Are the papers ready, Mr. Sullivan?"

"They sure are, Joey. Two cents per copy. They should sell out quickly."

"Soon as they do I'll be back lickety-split with the money. Thanks, Mr. Sullivan."

Joey grabbed a stack of papers and raced out the door. He started yelling "Extra!" before he reached the bottom of the stairs.

"To continue, I hope you understand my position, Vic. I'll crusade for law and order in Fort Griffin as long as necessary."

"That's admirable, Dale. In some ways you're more courageous than the bravest lawman or Indian fighter. You mind if I stick around for a while? I'm certain you'll have some unfriendly visitors before too long."

"Not at all. Be my guest. You don't mind if I clean up while you're here, do you?"

"Of course not."

Sullivan went to work, using solvent to clean ink off the lead type and the printing press's rolling plate. Vic busied himself observing activity on the street. Already several groups had formed, each gathered around a person holding a copy of the *Echo*.

Twenty minutes later, Joey ran back into the office.

"Every paper's sold, Mr. Sullivan. Seems like everyone wanted a copy."

"You did a good job, Joey. Thanks."

"Here's your money, Mr. Sullivan."

Sullivan took the coins Joey held out, then gave him twenty-five cents.

"And here's your pay, Joey."

"Twenty-five cents. That's too much. You give me a dime a week."

"But this was a special edition. Extra edition, extra pay."

"Gee whillikers! Thanks, Mr. Sullivan. Thanks a whole lot. My ma and pa will be so happy."

Joey ran back out. Vic watched a group of

people advancing up the street, heading for the *Echo*'s office.

"Here come the first of your visitors, Dale. They look none too happy."

Several men and two women burst into the newspaper office. Hap Wilkins, owner of the Griffin Guzzler, the town's largest saloon, was in the lead. He held a copy of the paper, which he crumpled and waved in Sullivan's face.

"How dare you print such trash, Sullivan? Stating that this town needs more law enforcement like last night, that Fort Griffin will prosper without our businesses. And you, Marshal. We're certainly happy to see you here. We as a group are sending a letter to Austin, demanding you be removed from your post immediately."

"Obviously you don't know Judge Canton. That won't work. If anything, it will make him even more determined to keep me assigned to Fort Griffin until it's settled down," Vic answered. "Y'all are so worried about the money you lost last night. First of all, from what I saw, business was pretty damn good. The best it's been in a long time. Second, there was no vandalism, no horses shot dead by a stray bullet from some drunken cowhand's gun, no innocent bystanders caught in the middle of a gunfight. Third, and most important, except for the SA Cross man who came after me, there were no serious injuries, and no deaths. That I believe speaks for itself."

"As far as I'm concerned, I'll keep crusading against the bad elements in this town," Sullivan said. "I don't intimidate easily. Unless y'all are here to report news, this conversation is over. If anyone is still here in two minutes, I'll ask Marshal Verdugo to arrest those persons for breach of peace and threatening. Is that clear?"

"It is. So's this. We'll shut you down, Sullivan. It's a long fall from that high horse you're on. You have my word on that. And Hap Wilkins always makes good on his word."

Vic pulled his pistol from its holster.

"You heard the man. Leave. Now."

"We're going," Wilkins said. "But this isn't finished yet. Not by a long shot."

"It better be," Vic said.

"We're not done with you yet either, Verdugo."

With that, Wilkins and the others left the office, slamming the door behind them.

"And so it begins," Sullivan said.

"And soon we'll find out how it ends," Vic answered. "Right now, I'm going to take a nap. I figure it will be a late night."

20

Two hours later, Vic was awakened by the sounds of breaking glass, running feet, and men shouting. He was surprised to notice the sun hadn't set. He jumped out of bed, stamped into his boots, buckled his gun belt around his waist, and grabbed a shotgun. He ran out of the office and dashed for the *Fort Griffin Echo*'s office. A mob was gathered in front, some throwing rocks through the windows and door while others were dragging the printing press and other equipment into the street.

One man held a torch, ready to toss it into the building. Vic didn't hesitate. He let loose with one barrel of the shotgun. Buckshot tore through the man's arm and hand, tearing the torch from his grasp. The torch fell. It flickered out in the dust. Its bearer staggered into a hitch rail and somersaulted over it, landing flat on his back, struggling for breath.

Vic fired the shotgun's second barrel, aiming low to cut the legs out from under several men. The mob's angry shouts turned to screams of pain and panic. Those who hadn't been hit took off running.

Dale Sullivan staggered out of the building. He had been severely beaten. His face was a mask of blood, his shirt torn off to reveal his back, chest, and abdomen bloodied and bruised. His left arm hung limply, clearly broken.

Two soldiers' wives who had been in town doing some shopping stopped dead in their tracks, across the street from the newspaper building.

"Do either of you ladies know where Doctor Taylor's office is located?" Vic yelled.

"I do," one said. "I'll hurry and fetch him."

"I'm a nurse," the other said. "I'll help tend to the wounded."

"I'm obliged, ladies."

Vic's first concern was Dale Sullivan. The newspaperman was walking around in a daze. Vic grabbed him by the shoulder and forced him to sit on the steps in front of his ruined office.

"Dale. Dale. It's me, Vic."

"Vic? Oh, Marshal Verdugo. I want to report a crime."

"No need. Not right now. You've got to get patched up first. Doc Taylor will be here soon."

Bobbi Jean, one of the ladies from the Fort Griffin Social Club, came running up.

"We can use my petticoats for bandages," she said, lifting her skirt and tearing strips from her undergarments. The Army wife, unfazed at the sight, kept working on the man she was aiding.

"Don't bump his arm," Vic cautioned Bobbi Jean. "It's busted. The doc will need to splint it."

"I'll be careful."

Bobbi Jean took a bright yellow silk handkerchief from her ample cleavage and began wiping blood and dirt from Sullivan's face.

"Dale, do you know who led this mob?" Vic asked.

"I don't know if they were the leaders, but two of the men who work at The Ruby Begonia were in front."

"Can you give me their names?"

"Just their first ones. Sloan, and an *hombre* who calls himself Brazos Bill."

"Was the owner with them?"

"Al Rawlins? He sure was."

"That gives me a good place to start."

Doctor Taylor, carrying his medical bag, hurried up.

"How bad is he, Marshal?"

"He's got a lot of scrapes, cuts, and bruises all over, but the worst injury is his left arm. It's busted."

"It can't be," Sullivan objected. "I've got to get my printing press back inside and put things back together. I need to get prepared for next week's regular paper."

"You won't be doing anything but taking it easy and mending for the next several weeks," Taylor told him. "Fort Griffin will have to do without a paper until you're healthy again."

"But that's exactly what the people who organized this raid want," Sullivan protested.

"Can't you understand that, Doc? If they put me out of business there will be no one in town who's a voice for law and common decency. I also can't have my press left out here in the street. The dust will get into it and render it unusable. And if it rains the press will rust, making it worthless. Even if I had the cash to order a replacement, which I don't, it could take months to arrive."

"Don't you worry about your stuff, Dale," Vic said. "I'll get a few men to help me put it back inside. We'll board up the windows until they can be replaced. As far as a paper, you still have use of your right arm. You can handwrite an issue and post it out front until you're up and around again."

"I . . . I don't know."

"Don't let the bastards win, Sugar," Bobbi Jean told Sullivan, with a sweet smile. "I'll help you. Stay with you until you're all healed up. I'm an excellent nurse. Particularly when it comes to bathing a feller."

"There you go, Dale. No more excuses," Taylor said. "Let me get to work on you."

"And let me get to work on my job," Vic added. "It's time to teach some people a lesson."

Vic checked on the wounded as he headed for Foster's Hardware. Most of the injuries were bloody, but not that serious. The torch bearer,

Cuddy Norton, who bartended at the Griffin Guzzler, was the most seriously hurt.

Vic had kept Jules Yankton and Hank Zee on as deputies. They were directing the people tending to the wounded. Vic was grateful for one thing. Soiled doves were working alongside respectable women, rough and tumble hide hunters alongside store owners. Fort Griffin had not yet developed into a town where the self-declared "better" classes would cross the street rather than speaking to those they considered their inferiors. Vic hoped it never would.

"Hank, you're in charge here. Any of these wounded men who don't have to remain at the doc's—put them in jail. Stay there until I get back. Jules, come with me."

"I'll be right with you, Marshal. Mrs. Slocum, this man is ready, except for the final bandaging."

"I'll take care of that, Mr. Yankton."

"Deputy Yankton," Vic corrected.

"Of course."

"Where are we headed?" Yankton asked, struggling to keep up with Vic's long strides.

"Foster's Hardware to get some tools. Then we'll pay a visit to the sons of bitches who tried to kill Dale Sullivan and burn him out."

"I'm right with you on that."

Bert Foster was standing in front of his store, holding a shotgun.

"Are things under control, Marshal?" he asked Vic.

"Mostly. I just have some clean-up work to finish. I need to purchase two sturdy axes and two sledgehammers. Put those on the State Government's account."

"Of course. I'll bring them right out."

"You're not one of those Temperance fanatics, are you?" Yankton asked Vic. "You know, like those crazy women who go around singing hymns and busting up taverns."

"Not normally, but sometimes I do make an exception," Vic answered. He smiled.

Yankton gave him a knowing grin.

Foster returned with the axes and sledgehammers.

"Here you are, Marshal. Planning on doing a little hunting?"

"That's the general idea, Bert," Vic said, as he hefted one of the axes. "These should do the trick."

"Good luck."

"Appreciate that."

Vic was a bit taken aback to see no one outside of the Ruby Begonia Saloon. Apparently the owner, and his employees and customers, figured Vic would still be busy in the center of town. They were about to find out just how mistaken they were. Vic had made the mistake of believing any attack would come under the cover of dark. It was a mistake he would never make again, and intended to make up for, right now.

Al Rawlins and five men were at the bar when Vic and Yankton walked in.

"Good evening, Marshal. What can I do for you this fine night?"

Rawlins smiled an unctuous smile. He was a fat man, packing well over two hundred pounds on a five foot seven frame. He was bald, but wore a huge set of burnsides. He was impeccably dressed in a white boiled shirt, green silk cravat held in place by a diamond stickpin, and black broadcloth trousers.

"Let's skip the niceties, Rawlins. Which of these men are Sloan and Brazos Bill?"

"Why, the two on either side of me. What do you want with them?"

"They're under arrest for attempted arson, attempted murder, assault, destruction of private property, breach of the peace and causing a riot."

"Why that's not possible. They've been here all afternoon. Nowhere near the newspaper office. Isn't that right, Sam?"

"Yes sir, Mr. Rawlins," the bartender agreed. "Just sitting around, playing cards and drinking whiskey."

"I see. Then perhaps I was mistaken. Although how did you know the trouble was at the newspaper?"

"Perhaps you were, Marshal. I heard about what happened. You know how word gets around in a small town. Tell you what. I'll buy you and Jules a drink. On the house. We can bury the hatchet, so to speak."

"Oh, I'm about to bury the hatchet, all right. As deep as I can into your big fat belly."

Before Rawlins could react, Vic reversed the axe he held, stalked up to the Ruby Begonia's owner, and buried its handle deep into the man's gut.

Rawlins jerked back, doubled over, and collapsed to the sawdust covered floor, gagging.

"Let's get to work, Jules."

Vic slammed the axe's handle against Brazos Bill's left side, breaking several of his ribs with an audible crack. Sam went for the sawed-off shotgun under the bar. When he brought it up, Vic chopped off its butt, breaking it in two, then slammed the axe against Sam's jaw, shattering it.

Jules drove his sledgehammer into Sloan's right knee, smashing the kneecap and felling Sloan like a tree. The other man, Ford Eaton, went for his six-gun. Jules swung the sledgehammer in a wide, horizontal arc, catching Eaton's hand between the sledge's heavy head and his hip. Every bone in Eaton's hand was smashed, his hip fractured. He fell heavily, howling, then passed out from pain and shock.

With Rawlins and his men out of commission,

Vic and Jules destroyed the interior of the Ruby Begonia. They chopped open beer barrels, swept all the whiskey bottles off the shelves behind the bar to smash on the floor. Jules picked up a chair and threw it against the back bar mirror, shattering it. He and Vic went through the saloon, chopping tables and chairs to bits. Their last act was to chop holes through the bar, then overturn it.

Rawlins had managed to drag some air back into his lungs.

"You . . . you won't get away . . . with this, Verdugo."

"Verdugo? Do you mean Marshal Verdugo? He ain't been down to this part of town all day. He's been dealing with the problem at the newspaper. Isn't that right, Deputy Yankton?"

"It sure is. He's been up there all afternoon. I just left him a few minutes ago. Plenty of folks will testify to that, too," Yankton said. He couldn't keep from laughing.

"You might want to send someone for Doc Taylor," Vic told Rawlins. "Of course, it might take him some time to get here. He's got a lot of hurt people he's tending to. But I'm certain he'll make it, eventually."

"That's right. Eventually," Yankton added.

"Time to go to our next stop," Vic said. "Oh, by the way Rawlins, your establishment is officially and permanently closed."

• • •

Unlike at the Ruby Begonia, seven men including Hap Wilkins, the owner, were waiting in front of the Griffin Guzzler.

"You don't want to start something you can't finish, Marshal," Wilkins said.

"Is that any way to greet the man who just put your biggest competitor out of business, Wilkins?"

"You mean . . . ?"

"Yup. The Ruby Begonia. Why don't you saunter down there and have a looksee?"

"And for what reason would I want to do that?"

"To see what your place is about to look like."

"Damn you to Hell, Marshal. Men, stop him."

Vic and Yankton each had a shotgun, in addition to the axes and sledgehammers they carried. In place of the normal load of buckshot, they had loaded the scatterguns with rock salt and horseshoe nails.

Only one of Wilkins' men managed to clear leather before he and the others were cut down. His six-gun fired once, putting a bullet into his own foot.

"Kind of bloody business, isn't it?" Yankton asked.

"Yeah, but at least we haven't killed anyone yet," Vic answered. "Although some of them might not pull through."

"Damn you, Marshal! Stay the hell out of my

saloon," Wilkins yelled. He was lying in the street, his trouser legs torn and bloody.

"Don't worry. We won't stay long," Vic assured him.

He and Yankton went inside the Griffin Guzzler. They repeated their actions from the Ruby Begonia. All the beer barrels were chopped open, the whiskey bottles smashed, the gambling tables destroyed. Not a stick of furniture was left undamaged.

Wilkins and his cronies were still lying in the street.

"I'll send Doc Taylor down to you, soon as he finishes taking care of Dale Sullivan and a few other injured innocent bystanders. Also, just like the Ruby Begonia, your hellhole is officially and permanently closed."

21

With Fort Griffin quiet after the raid on the newspaper, and the shuttering of two of the town's most infamous saloons, Vic decided to take the opportunity to have a well-deserved haircut, shave, and bath. Besides, next to a saloon, the barber shop was inevitably the best source for the latest information and gossip.

Since Topper also needed new shoes, Vic rode him over to Tom Jensen's blacksmith and farrier shop.

"Good morning, Marshal. Nice day, ain't it?" Jensen greeted him. Jensen was blonde haired and gray eyed, like most farriers shirtless and muscular under the canvas trousers and leather apron he wore. He was filing the left front hoof of a big blaze-faced chestnut draft horse.

"It sure is, Tom," Vic agreed. "Topper needs to be reshod, and I need a good currying myself. Do you mind if I leave him with you while I head on over to the barber shop?"

"Not at all. My holding corral is empty. Put him in there and toss him some hay. There's a water bucket you can fill for him, too."

"I'm obliged. C'mon, Topper, let's go."

Vic led his stallion to the small corral behind the smithy, which was shaded by a good-sized cottonwood tree. He took the saddle, blanket, and bridle off Topper, hanging them on the fence. He slipped a halter on the horse's head, and left a lead rope for Tom by the corral's gate. After filling the water bucket, tossing some hay into the corral, and giving his horse a piece of licorice, Vic made the short walk to the elegantly named Frenchy's Tonsorial and Bathing Emporium. There were no other customers when he walked inside.

"Good mornin', Marshal," Frenchy LeDoux greeted him. "I figured it was about time I'd be seeing you for a haircut."

"You figured right, Frenchy," Vic answered, as he took off his hat and hung it from a peg. "Although it'll probably be more like a sheep shearing than a haircut and shave. I'll be wanting a bath, too."

"I wasn't even going to ask you that," Frenchy answered. "It was obvious the minute you walked through the door."

"I guess I do smell plenty rank, at that."

Vic settled in the shop's lone chair. Frenchy adjusted it to match the marshal's height, then draped a clean white cloth over him and knotted it at the nape of his neck. Vic, for his part, had taken his Smith and Wesson from its holster and held it in his lap, ready for use if necessary.

"How short do you want your hair cut?" Frenchy asked.

"So short I won't even need to part it."

"What about your beard and moustache?"

"I want them gone. They'll grow back quick enough anyway."

"Then I'll get to work."

Frenchy took a pair of shears to remove most of Vic's hair, and its many knots. He then took a lighter pair of scissors to trim Vic's hair evenly all around. He jabbered all the while he was working. Before he was finished, Vic would know every last piece of gossip in town.

"Looks like that Bobbi Jean has moved right in with Dale Sullivan. She always did have a sweet spot for him. Mark my words, they'll be married before too long. I dunno, a respectable gent like Mr. Sullivan hitching up with a loose woman like Bobbi Jean."

"He could do worse," Vic said. "He could marry a nice, well-bred society lady who turns out to be a shrew. End up spending the rest of his life henpecked. It's not the station in life that counts, it's the person."

"I suppose you're right at that, Marshal."

Frenchy held a mirror behind Vic's head.

"How's that look, Marshal?"

"It looks just fine, Frenchy."

"Good. Now let me get at that beard. It's so long and tangled I'm surprised a prairie wren hasn't built a nest in it."

"I keep movin' fast enough so they can't," Vic said, with a chuckle.

Frenchy kept chattering while he stropped his razor, then mixed up a mug of shaving soap. He began lathering Vic's face.

"Are you worried about the saloonkeepers, gambling parlor operators, and brothel owners setting up their own district, and bringing in their own law?"

Vic's ears perked up. This was one piece of information which hadn't reached him.

"What do you mean?"

"A whole bunch of them got together for a meeting last night. They plan on declaring their part of town its own district. They'll be hiring their own lawmen. They think they can override your authority that way."

"They can think whatever they want. Texas law overrides local law. And until Reconstruction is completely revoked, Federal law overrules Texas law."

"The people behind it think they'll get enough support to run you out of town if you fight them."

"They'd better be careful what they wish for. If I pull out, the Army will declare martial law and move in. That will shut just about everything down. It also suspends all sorts of Constitutional rights."

"Marshal, please. You didn't hear this from me."

"Not a word," Vic assured the worried barber, whose hand was now shaking. He really didn't care for having his throat accidentally sliced open.

Realizing he might have said too much, and to the wrong person, Frenchy went silent. He shaved off Vic's thick, tangled beard without saying another word.

"That will be thirty cents, Marshal," he said, as he removed the apron covering Vic, shook it out, then brushed off Vic's neck and shoulders.

"Not quite yet," Vic said. "Did you forget I also came in for a bath?"

"Oh my gosh, Marshal. You're right. I should have started heating the water when you first got here. I'll get on it right now. It will just take a little while."

"I'm in no hurry."

Frenchy disappeared behind the curtain separating the bathing room from the rest of the shop. Vic settled in a chair and half-dozed while he waited. Half an hour later Frenchy reappeared.

"Your tub's filled, Marshal. I left plenty of soap, a washcloth, and towels for you."

"I'm much obliged, Frenchy. I'm going to take a good, long soak."

"Enjoy yourself."

Vic went into the back room, where awaited a long zinc tub filled almost to the brim with steaming hot water. He pulled a chair next to the tub, took off his boots and socks, then his gun belt and the rest of his clothing. He piled everything except the boots on the chair, leaving his gun on top, within easy reach if needed.

He got into the tub, sank all the way so only his head, neck, and knees were visible. It always amazed him how many aches he didn't realize he had until a tub of hot water began to soak them away. Being a lawman aged a man before his time.

Vic soaked for thirty minutes, then scrubbed himself, got out of the tub, toweled off, and redressed.

"You look real fine, Marshal," Frenchy said, when Vic came back out front. "Like a new man. Would you care for a splash of bay rum? It will only cost another five cents. It tightens the skin, and the ladies love the scent."

"Sure, why not? Thank you."

Frenchy took a bottle from off the shelf, poured some of the contents into his hands, then slapped them on Vic's cheeks. The liquid made his skin tingle.

"There you are, Marshal. That will be forty cents, all told."

Vic took two quarters from his pocket and handed them to the barber.

"You're all set, Frenchy. Keep the change. Now I'd better get over to Jensen's smithy and see if he's done reshoeing Topper. My horse gets a mite restless if I leave him for too long."

"Thanks, Marshal. Thanks a lot. You have a good rest of your day, now."

"You too, Frenchy. See you later."

Topper was tied to the hitch rail out front when Vic returned to the blacksmith. He whinnied a noisy greeting when he spotted his rider.

"All right, pard. I didn't leave you for all that long."

Tom Jensen came out of his shop.

"Your horse is all set, Marshal. That will be five dollars."

"Boy howdy, everything is getting so damned expensive," Vic said, as he took out his billfold, removed a five-dollar greenback, and handed it to the farrier.

"I know. It's the fault of those damn sons of bitches industrialists back East. The steel magnates have a monopoly on the iron ore. The coal magnates have a monopoly on coal. The railroads have a monopoly on transportation. So they all get together in their fancy clubs, sitting in leather chairs, sipping the best whiskey and expensive Cuban or Connecticut River Valley cigars, and price folks like you and me straight into poverty. It's not right, but they hold all the cards."

"Someday things might change, Tom."

Vic untied Topper, replaced the halter and lead rope with his bridle, and resaddled him.

“High time I took a *pasear* around town, Tom. See you later.”

“You be careful, Marshal.”

Vic answered with a wave, as he eased Topper into a walk.

22

Vic turned Topper straight in the direction of the bad side of Fort Griffin. Of course, in such a town, bad side was a term used loosely. Fort Griffin really had no good side.

He rode slowly between the saloons, gambling parlors, and brothels which lined both sides of the street. He looked directly at anyone who took a glance at him. Most of those averted their eyes, unable to meet the glittering icy green of Vic's gaze.

Word spread quickly that the marshal had returned, for the first time since his raid on the Ruby Begonia and Griffin Guzzler saloons. Both of those establishments had men inside, working on rebuilding them.

Vic gave a low, wry chuckle.

"Just as I figured. It didn't take long for those boys to start getting ready for business again. The next couple of weeks should prove mighty interesting."

Hap Wilkins rolled up to the Griffin Guzzler in a buggy pulled by matched bay mares, driven by a pale featured man.

"You've got a lot of guts, Marshal, showing yourself around here. I'll give you that. Well, it won't be long until you're leaving Fort Griffin with your tail between your legs . . . or in a pine box.”

“Are you talking about your little scheme to declare this part of Fort Griffin a separate entity, with its own laws and law enforcement, Wilkins?”

Wilkins looked startled. His mouth opened and shut like a fish out of water.

“Yeah, I’ve heard about it,” Vic said. “There’s not much that goes on in this town which I don’t hear about. That’s how a lawman stays alive. You might want to keep in mind if I go, the Army moves in. Since you don’t like my way of running a town, I can guarantee you’ll downright despise what happens when Colonel Elliott takes over.”

“Anyone can talk big, Marshal.”

“That’s right, Wilkins. Even you.”

Vic turned Topper and loped away, leaving Wilkins staring at his back.

Vic rode around town for an hour or so, then past the fort and up along the Clear Fork. He let Topper set his own pace, since he wasn’t headed in any particular direction. They wandered about, stopping every so often to rest.

Vic had ridden into an area of thicker vegetation along the river when he heard several shots.

“We’d better see what that’s all about, Topper.”

He spurred the stallion out of the brush and

onto the surrounding plain. Two Indians were lying dead in the grass, with bullet holes in their backs. Another Indian was huddled in the tall grass, his hands over the back of his head. Two white men holding rifles were riding up to them. A hundred yards off lay a dead antelope, with two arrows in its side.

Vic unshipped his Winchester and fired a shot just over the white men's heads. They whipped their horses around, to find themselves staring into the unwavering barrel of Vic's Yellowboy.

"Don't make a move," Vic warned. "I don't even want to see one of your horses switch his tail at a fly. United States Deputy Marshal Victor Verdugo. Now tell me what the hell's going on here. And you'd better have a damn good explanation."

"We've been killin' us some damn Indians who've been raiding our ranch's beef," the nearer man said.

Vic nodded at the two bodies lying in the grass, and the third Indian, who had gotten to his knees and was sobbing.

"These Indians? There isn't one of them more than fourteen years old."

"They're Injuns, ain't they?" the other man said. "That's all you need to know. Our boss, George Hopper, who owns the Hopping H Ranch, pays a five-dollar bounty for every scalp we bring in."

"Even young'uns like these?"

Vic spoke to the terrified surviving Indian in his native Comanche. The boy managed to get out his version of events.

"What'd he say, Marshal?" the closest man asked.

"He says he and his brothers were out hunting pronghorns, because the meat they get on the reservation is rotten. Says their family is starving."

"He's a damn liar! All Indians are."

"That looks a lot more like a pronghorn rather than a steer lyin' over there," Vic said. "It appears I'm gonna have to arrest you men for murder. I'm gonna have to pay a call on your boss, too."

"For shooting damn Indians?"

Both men went to trigger their rifles. Vic shot each in the center of the chest, knocking them both off their horses.

Vic got off Topper, and called to the young Indian brave, again speaking in Comanche.

"What is your name?"

"Cloud Dancer."

"If I help you get your brothers' bodies back on their horses, will you be able to take them home? I will also put the pronghorn on your horse."

The young man stood proudly erect.

"Yes."

"Good."

Vic got the two young men's bodies on their

horses and lashed them in place. He tied the pronghorn behind one of them.

"One more thing."

Vic scalped the two killers, and handed their scalps to the boy.

"You and your brothers counted coup before they were killed. Do you understand?"

"Yes."

"Good. It will be best to have them remembered as brave warriors. I am certain if these evil men had not shot them in the back, from hiding, you and your brothers would have fought well. Take them home where they can be mourned, and honored."

"I will."

Once Cloud Dancer was on his way, Vic loaded the two dead bushwhackers on their horses, tying them belly down over their saddles.

"Now to have a chat with one Mr. George Hopper."

It only took about twenty minutes for Vic to reach the Hopping H Ranch. Two cowboys in front of the stable yelled and pointed when they saw him coming. A man came from inside the barn to join them. All three watched as Vic rode up.

"Those my two men you got there, Marshal?" the man who'd come from inside the barn asked.

"United States Deputy Marshal Victor Verdugo. Are you George Hopper?"

"I am."

Hopper was in his early forties, skin bronzed by the Texas sun and wind, with brown hair and hard brown eyes. He had a week's worth of whiskers stubbling his face and neck. Just about five foot eight and one hundred seventy pounds, he was a typical hard-bitten Texas rancher.

"Then these are."

"Lousy bastard Indians scalped them? Did you get the men who did this?"

"No Comanches or Kiowas did this. You're looking at the man who did."

Vic didn't give Hopper the opportunity to break in as he continued speaking.

"These men backshot two young Comanche boys from ambush, and were fixing to kill a third when I happened upon them. They tried to claim those boys were rustling Hopping H beef. What they'd killed was a pronghorn they were going to take home to their starving family. When I told your men they were under arrest for murder, they went for their guns. A mistake they'll never make again."

"You killed two of my top hands over a few stinking Indians?" Hopper shouted.

"I sure did. Scalped them, too. But mostly because they tried to kill me. Funny thing is if they'd just submitted to arrest they'd most likely have ended up being turned loose. I doubt there's any jury in Texas which would take the word of an Indian, or a black man, over a white's. I told the one brother they hadn't killed to tell his family that his kin had counted coup before they were gunned down by a pair of cowards, and gave him their scalps."

"I'll have your badge for this, Marshal!"

"You can try, but I doubt it. I came here to place you under arrest for conspiracy to commit murder. However, with no witnesses except two dead ones, I don't have a case. So I'm going to leave you with a warning. As best as I can, I'll be keeping watch on you. Your dead men there told me you were paying five dollars a scalp bounty. That's illegal, not to mention damned immoral. Anyone with black hair, Indian or not, would be likely to lose their hair to unscrupulous hunters. So keep your men in check from here on out, or expect another visit from me. The next one won't be so friendly."

Vic dropped the reins of the horses carrying the dead men, then, rifle in hand, backed Topper out of the Hopping H yard. He turned the horse and loped him back toward Fort Griffin. He doubted he'd heard the last of George Hopper, but there was always hope common sense would prevail. Not likely in Texas, but the chance was still there.

23

Vic was in his office two days later when a commotion broke out in the street. He hurried outside to see what had caused all the excitement.

People were standing in groups, the entire length of the street abuzz in conversation. Vic stopped and joined two storekeepers from the Fort Griffin Mercantile.

"What's all the excitement, John? Did Molly Pickett leave her curtains open again? That woman does love to put on a show."

"No, Marshal. Ain't you heard? Wyatt Earp just came into town."

"Wyatt Earp, the former Dodge City lawman? Not to mention pimp and card shark?"

"Yep, sure enough. Rode right through town big as life and stopped at the Occidental Hotel. It seems as if he's decided to put down stakes here in Fort Griffin."

"Word has it Doc Holliday is on his way, too," Dave Massey, John Fergus's partner, said. "Maybe even Bat Masterson. Big Nose Kate is supposed to be coming along too. They'll sure put Fort Griffin on the map."

"Not in a good way," Vic muttered.

"What was that, Marshal?" Massey said.

"What? Oh, nothing. Just thinking out loud."

"Aren't you goin' to see him, Marshal?" Fergus asked. "Give him a proper like welcome and all that. Show him around the town, make him feel at home?"

"I reckon not. If Mr. Earp has any desire or need to see me, he'll work his way to my office, sooner or later. In the meantime, I'm heading for a meeting with Colonel Elliott. You boys take care now."

He left the two men staring at his back while he went to saddle Topper.

"Boy howdy, our marshal sure don't seem impressed Wyatt Earp is here in Fort Griffin," Massey said.

"He's probably afraid of him. Or maybe he thinks Earp is after his job," Fergus answered.

"Well, none of that's our worry. Let's go down to the hotel and see if we can catch a glimpse of Mr. Earp."

The sentry at the gate recognized Vic, or more likely his distinctive Medicine Hat stallion.

"Halt, Marshal," he ordered, after Vic had already reined Topper to a stop.

"Good morning, Private."

"Good morning, sir. What might I do for you?"

"Would Colonel Elliott be available? Something's come up that I need to discuss with him."

"I'm not certain. You may pass. His aide will let you know if the colonel can spare a few minutes."

"Thank you, Private. I'm obliged."

Vic put Topper into an easy walk, rode across what passed for the parade ground in the still-to-be and never-would-be completed fort, then stopped at Colonel Elliott's office. He dismounted, gave Topper a piece of licorice, looped his reins around the hitch rail, then went inside.

Lieutenant Stanton was at his desk.

"Good morning, Marshal Verdugo. Was the colonel expecting you today? I don't have you on his calendar."

"He wasn't, because I had no plans to be here today. However, something has come up he needs to hear about. I'll only need about ten minutes of his time."

"Let me go ask him."

Stanton disappeared into Elliott's office. He reappeared a moment later and gestured to Vic to head down the hall.

"Colonel Elliott says he has fifteen minutes to spare."

"That's more than I'll need."

Elliott was already standing when Vic entered his office.

"Good morning, Marshal. To what do I owe the pleasure of this visit? Would you care for coffee, or a cigar?"

Vic shook his head.

"Both sound good, but I haven't got the time. Your aide tells me you're also quite busy. I'll get right to the point. Wyatt Earp is in town."

"Wyatt Earp? Here? In Fort Griffin?"

"I haven't seen him personally, but he's here all right. Did you know anything about this?"

"Not until you just told me. I would have notified you if I had. I wonder what brings Earp to Fort Griffin?"

"Money. I'm certain you're aware besides being a lawman he's owned brothels, gambling parlors, and saloons. He's quite the gambler. What better place to try his luck than here?"

"It seems he could find a larger town to ply his trade."

"You're right, Colonel. Rumors are flying, of course. Folks are saying Doc Holliday and maybe Bat Masterson are coming to join him."

"A holy, or unholy, triumvirate, depending on your opinion of those three."

"Correct. I have an idea why Earp has shown up here. Hap Wilkins and some of the other business owners are trying to declare their part of town a separate entity, with its own law enforcement. That's exactly the type of situation where the Earps and their friends like to step in and have themselves appointed as the law."

"That would never be declared legal in the legislature, or by a court of law."

"No, it wouldn't. But there could be an awful lot of trouble in the meantime."

"What might you be needing from me, or my troops?"

"Hopefully nothing. All we can do is wait and see what happens. Earp, and the others if they indeed arrive, might just remain here a few days, then move on to someplace with bigger pickings. So for now we watch and wait. If Wilkins and his friends try to take over Fort Griffin, that's when I'll ask you for assistance."

"That would necessitate declaring martial law."

"Let's hope it doesn't come to that."

"Indeed. I have fewer men than usual here at the moment. I sent out a patrol looking for Comanches who have been raiding local ranches."

"Let me guess. The complaint was filed by George Hopper of the Hopping H Ranch."

"That's correct. How did you know?"

"Because I discovered those so-called Comanche raiders myself. They were three boys, none over thirteen or fourteen years old. They were hunting antelope to feed their families. They had downed a pronghorn when two of Hopper's men shot two of them from ambush, in the back. They were going to kill the third until I stopped them. It seems Hopper was paying a five-dollar bounty for each Indian scalp turned over to him."

"I see. What happened to the men?"

“They resisted arrest. I had to kill them. Let the surviving boy take his brothers back home, while I took Hopper’s hired killers back to him. I didn’t have the evidence to bring him in on a murder conspiracy charge. I did warn him what would happen if he or his men were found hunting scalps again.”

“So it still won’t hurt to have a patrol out there. Although the men might be dealing with renegade whites, not Indians.”

“That’s correct, Colonel. I know you’re busy, and I’ve got to get back to town. I’ll see myself out.”

“Thank you. And keep me posted.”

24

The next afternoon, Vic was in his office when a man entered. He recognized him immediately.

"Howdy, Marshal. I'm Wyatt Earp."

"Good afternoon, Mr. Earp. I recognized you from several photographs. I'm United States Deputy Marshal Victor Verdugo."

"I'm pleased to make your acquaintance, Marshal. Do you have a few minutes to spare, so we can talk?"

"I've got all the time in the world. Take a seat. Smoke if you wish to."

"Thank you."

Earp took a seat, lit a thin cigar and took a long puff, while Vic rolled and lit a quirly.

"Now, what did you wish to discuss, Mr. Earp?"

"The law situation here in Fort Griffin. The South Fort Griffin Business Owners Association has employed myself and some of my associates to enforce the law in that section of town, independently of the rest of the city."

"I see. I assume your associates will include your brothers, perhaps Doc Holliday or Bat Masterson."

"You are partially correct. My brothers Virgil and Morgan are otherwise occupied up in Kansas at this time. My brother James prefers not to partake in enforcing the law. He and his wife are much more interested in caring for the wayward young women they have taken under their wings."

"Wayward young women."

"Yes. Wayward young women. To finish answering your question, yes, both Doc and Bat will be arriving within the next few days. Then we will take over law enforcement in South Fort Griffin."

"I see."

Vic leaned forward, put his elbows on the desk, then tented his hands in front of his face.

"I'm only going to speak once, so listen carefully, *Wyatt.* There is no such locality as South Fort Griffin. I, along with two men I hired as part-time deputies, enforce the laws in this town. If needed I can call in troops from the fort. The men who hired you have no legal standing to appoint you peace officers, and you have no power of arrest or any other powers granted to peace officers. If your employers want to hire you as security for their establishments, that's fine. Hell, if a fight breaks out and you or your partners have to break it up, that's fine. But if you, or anyone working with you, guns someone down, or assaults someone under the guise of law, you will be arrested and charged with the appropriate crime. That includes murder. You have *absolutely no legal authority* to act as peace officers here. Have I made myself clear?"

"You have indeed, Marshal. However, you know my reputation. I am not easily cowed."

"And in case you don't know what Verdugo translates to in English, it's Executioner. That's a nickname I've been hung with, and much as I hate it, sometimes it's damn accurate. My advice to you is leave Fort Griffin and avoid an awful lot of trouble."

"I'm afraid I can't do that, Marshal. Mr. Wilkins has already offered myself and my associates a forty percent stake in the Griffin Guzzler. I understand he's invited Big Nose Kate to become one of the house gamblers, along with Doc Holliday. They'll clean up. That's too much money for us to pass up."

"Of course. Your idea of enforcing the law includes skimming off the top of the businesses you're hired to protect. Then stick to gambling, boozing, and whoring and everything will be fine. But get in my way, and you'll be in jail, or dead."

"Big words, Marshal."

"Which I can back up. Good day, Mr. Earp."

When Earp reached the door and opened it, Vic let out a loud belch. Earp turned and glared at him.

"Beg pardon," said Vic.

25

Three days later, Big Nose Kate came into town, driving a fancy leather carriage pulled by two matched black geldings. She went right to work as a house gambler at the Griffin Guzzler.

Two days after Kate's arrival, Doc Holliday and Bat Masterson rode into Fort Griffin. As had Earp, they took up residence at the Occidental Hotel. All three went to work as ersatz city marshals. They kept out of trouble by making no arrests, simply disabling troublemakers with their fists or a gun barrel cracked on the skull, then keeping them overnight and sending them on their way in the morning, heads throbbing. Of course, Earp, Masterson, and Holliday did more than their fair share of gambling. They really didn't want to kill the goose which laid the golden eggs of gambling profits by stirring up the ire of Marshal Verdugo. And Holliday had become enamored of Big Nose Kate, spending every minute he could with the woman who would later become his common law wife until his death from tuberculosis.

Vic had put both Jules Yankton and Hank Zee on as full time deputies. The three of them were able to cover all of Fort Griffin, with no assistance from the Army.

"Y'know, Vic," Zee said one evening. "Things

have been a lot quieter around here since Earp and his friends arrived. Do you reckon things will stay that way?"

"Let's hope so, but I doubt it," Vic answered. "Time for me to take over. Go get some rest, Hank."

"That's exactly what I'm planning on."

Zee hadn't been gone ten minutes when he came racing back into the office, out of breath.

"Marshal, we've got real trouble down by the Griffin Guzzler. What just happened I've been told is Jules went to arrest one of Wilkins' men after he beat a cowboy to pulp. The man pulled a gun, so Jules had to shoot him. He's dead. Wyatt Earp's arrested Jules. He's planning on holding a trial right now."

"With a jury of the saloon's customers," Vic said, grabbing his hat and jamming it on his head. "They'll hang Jules if we don't hurry."

Vic pulled a shotgun from the rack. Topper was already out front and tied, saddle in place.

"Borrow that sorrel, Hank," he ordered Zee, indicating a horse tied alongside Topper. "We'll explain to its owner later."

Zee untied the sorrel and swung into the saddle.

"Let's go."

When they arrived at the entertainment district, Yankton was on the porch of the Griffin Guzzler, his hands tied behind his back. Earp, Holliday, and Masterson were with him, along with Hap Wilkins and three of his employees. A mob was gathered in front of the saloon, some already holding up ropes and calling for the deputy's lynching.

Vic pulled Topper to a sliding stop and fired one barrel of the shotgun over the crowd, instantly grabbing their attention.

"Earp, you'd better turn my deputy loose. *Now!*"

"I can't do that, Marshal. He's been arrested for a cold-blooded killing."

"By whom?"

"Me is whom."

"You were warned you have no legal authority in Texas, Earp. Same goes for your pals, Masterson and Holliday. If someone has cause to press charges, they'll need to speak with me. Otherwise, turn my deputy loose or I'll come take him from you."

Doc Holliday snorted, a mean, derisive laugh.

"Do you really think just the two of you can stand up against us, and the rest of these fine citizens, who intend to see justice done?"

"Make that three."

Dale Sullivan, unnoticed, had joined Vic and Zee. The newspaperman held a double-barreled shotgun.

"I don't just think so, I know so," Vic answered.

"He's just bluffing, Wyatt," Masterson said.

"Try me."

"Don't worry about Verdugo, Wyatt," Holliday said. "I've got him. I'm your huckleberry."

"You have one chance to give up my man, and for this mob to disperse," Vic said. "Otherwise, my play goes like this. Holliday, I know you've got a shotgun hidden under that duster coat of yours. You've always been a four-flusher and a coward. So my first shot will be aimed right at the scattergun. It'll hit it, you can bet your hat on that, because I don't miss what I aim at . . . *ever!* The charges will explode, and blow your damn huckleberries clean off. Then I'll sink a couple of slugs into you, Earp. Finally, I'll blow that stupid looking derby hat clean off Masterson's head with a bullet through his forehead. By then one of you might have gotten me, but that won't matter because y'all will be dead. So will those reputations as hard-nosed lawmen you've been working so hard to build, while bilking as much money as you can out of anywhere you set up shop."

"As for the rest of you, soon as any shooting starts my other deputy here, and Mr. Sullivan whom I am of this moment appointing special deputy, will empty their shotguns into the whole damn bunch of you, with special emphasis on cutting down you and your gunfighters, Wilkins. Every last one of you knows the damage a shotgun can do. Who wants to take the chance he won't catch a slug and be lying dead in the street when the shooting stops?"

A few people at the edges of the mob started slinking away. They wanted no part of taking a load of buckshot.

"Earp, do what I'm paying you for!" Wilkins ordered.

"I *was* hired to do a job, Marshal," Earp said.

"That job includes lynching? Lynching a United States Special Deputy Marshal at that?"

Earp shrugged.

"The man does raise a valid point, Mr. Wilkins," he said. "This isn't exactly the picture you painted when you contacted us. Sometimes a man has to know when to throw in a bad hand. It seems as if this is one of those times. Bat, untie the deputy and let him go. Mr. Wilkins, my associates and I hereby resign. Marshal Verdugo, we'll leave town first thing tomorrow morning."

"You made the right decision."

"I'm not certain. We probably could have outgunned you. But the odds at least one of us would have died in the process were too high. As you've said, I'm a gambler. A good gambler knows when he's beat. You win."

The spectators were stunned at the sudden, unexpected turn of events. They had just witnessed United States Deputy Marshal Victor V. Verdugo face down three of the West's most notorious gunmen. And he'd done so without firing a shot. Almost silently, they began breaking up. Even Hap Wilkins and his men went back into the Griffin Guzzler, shaking their heads.

"Thanks for saving my bacon, Marshal," Yankton said, once he was with Vic and the others.

"It might not be saved yet," Vic cautioned. "I won't be satisfied this is over until Earp and friends leave town."

26

Vic was awakened four nights later by someone attempting to break into his office. The night was hot and humid, so he was sleeping in only his denim trousers. As the person kept working at the door, Vic slipped out of bed. Not wanting to take a chance of bumping into something in the dark, possibly alerting the intruder he knew of his presence and was lying in wait, he didn't put on a shirt or pull on his boots. He strapped his gun belt around his waist, put a bullet into the empty chamber under the hammer, then padded barefoot across the office to the door.

The intruder kicked in the door just as Vic reached it. Despite being surprised to see the marshal standing right there in front of him, not asleep in bed, he still fired the gun he held in his left hand, at the same moment Vic pulled the trigger of his Smith and Wesson.

A red-hot iron poker seemed to ram its way through Vic's belly. His attacker's eyes opened wide, his moon face crossed with an expression of shock and pain when Vic's bullet tore into his chest. He dropped, to reveal another man behind him. Even as he clutched at his bullet torn gut and started to fold, Vic put a bullet into the second man's stomach. Three more men burst out of the night.

A second bullet creased Vic's right ribs, his return shot catching the shooter in the throat. Blood spurted from his ruptured jugular vein. He staggered into the street and fell.

Vic had fallen onto his side, helpless against the two remaining men. He braced himself for the impact of more hot lead tearing through him. Several shots rang out from the street. The last two men fell, their backs riddled with bullets. The hoofbeats of a single galloping horse rapidly faded into the distance.

Jules Yankton and Hank Zee hurried over to Vic, who had rolled onto his back.

"Marshal, how bad are you hit?" Yankton asked.

Zee said, "Sorry we couldn't get here sooner. We were called to a disturbance at the Honey Bee. Came a-runnin' when we heard the shots. One of 'em got away."

"Bad. Real bad. Gut-shot. Better get Doc Taylor. And send someone up to the fort. Rouse Colonel Elliott. It seems his aide was making some money on the side."

The first man Vic had shot was Lieutenant Jeremiah Stanton. He was now lying on his back, blood pooling around him, eyes wide open in the unblinking stare of death.

Next to Stanton, also staring blankly at the waxing gibbous moon, lay the mortal remains of Hap Wilkins.

27

Vic awakened a week later, to the mingled odors of medicines and soaps. He could feel the pressure of a bandage wrapped around his middle. His eyes flickered open. It took him a moment to realize he was lying in a bed at Doctor Taylor's.

Hank Zee was sitting in a chair alongside Vic's bed, with a shotgun leaning against the wall next to him.

"Marshal! You're awake. Let me get Doc Taylor."

"Send for Colonel Elliott too. I've gotta talk to him quick, in case I don't make it."

"You're gonna pull through. Doc already said so. But I'll get the colonel."

Once Zee left, Vic dozed back off until he heard Doctor Taylor come into the room.

"Howdy, Doc. You sure ain't no angel, so I guess I haven't died and gone to Heaven."

He managed a weak chuckle.

"You came closer to meeting St. Peter at the Pearly Gates than you realize, Marshal," Taylor answered, clearly not amused. "I had to do extensive reconstructive surgery inside your abdomen. Your surviving is nothing short of a miracle. That you were able to fight off the infection was even more miraculous."

"Do you mean I'm going to be all right?"

"Unless some unexpected setback occurs, yes. I would have thought if that was going to happen it would have by now. You will be laid up for a month or so. Healing your insides will be a slow process."

"And here I thought I'd be dancing next week."

"Could you ever dance, Marshal?"

"No. Not really."

"And you still won't be able to. I'm going to change the dressings and replace the bandages now. I should be finished by the time Colonel Elliott arrives. I can't allow you much time with him. You still need a lot of rest."

Taylor had just finished replacing Vic's bandages when Hank Zee returned, along with Jules Yankton and Colonel Elliott.

"No hand shaking," Taylor warned. "That could pass dirt and germs. Y'all have fifteen minutes, tops. No more."

Colonel Elliott settled for a smile.

"It's good to see you awake, Marshal. Doctor Taylor told me your survival was touch and go. I'm happy to see you're looking quite well, for a man who was at death's door."

"Thank you, Colonel. It's good to see you also."

"Fifteen minutes," Taylor reminded them.

"I guess you'd better fill me in on the details of what happened the other night, Colonel," Vic said. "Why did your aide join Hap Wilkins in the attempt on my life?"

Elliott shook his head.

"Lieutenant Stanton was a good man with a bad problem, a gambling one. He got in over his head with both Wilkins and Miss Bee at her place. I had been having him watched for quite some time now, because he was embezzling funds from the government. Apparently even those couldn't cover his debts, so when Wilkins offered him the opportunity to clean the slate by killing you, he took the bait."

"Excuse me, but how do you know all this? I shot both Stanton and Wilkins dead. They damn for certain didn't do any talking."

"Stanton's confederate, Sergeant Raul Escobar. He's the other soldier who was with Wilkins that night. He was captured, and is being held at the fort's stockade. He'll face a court-martial."

"Wrap it up, gentlemen," Taylor warned.

"We can go over things in more detail at another time, Marshal. Suffice it to say Fort Griffin is as peaceful right now as it ever will be. How long that will last, *quien sabe*? Judge Canton has authorized the Army to enforce the law in Fort Griffin until you are able to return to duty. Your two deputies here will do most of the work, unless a situation calls for more manpower. Then the Army will step in. The order expires in sixty days."

"What happens after sixty days?"

Elliott gave a soft laugh.

"Either you'll be back to work, or dead."

"Here I thought Dale Sullivan had a sick sense of humor," Vic said, also laughing. "Yours is even worse."

"Gentlemen, I hate to stop you here, but I have to insist you leave. I can't allow the marshal to overtax himself."

"All right, Doc," Yankton said. "Vic, is there anything you need before we go?"

"As a matter of fact, there is. Where are my personal possessions?"

"In the top drawer in that chest," Taylor answered, pointing at an old oak bureau.

"Would one of you get my rosary beads, please?"

"Rosary beads?" Yankton echoed.

"Yes. Catholics like me use them to pray to the Blessed Virgin Mary to intercede before God for us, and to give thanks for favors granted. I can't think of a bigger request granted than my life not being taken by a point-blank shot to my gut. The beads were in my vest pocket, in a small black velvet pouch."

"I remember those," Taylor said. "I took them out of the pocket and placed them on top of the chest. I wasn't certain what they were, but somehow I knew you would want them."

"I'll get them," Yankton said.

Yankton took the pouch from the chest and handed it to Vic. Vic removed the rosaries and kissed the feet of Jesus on the crucifix.

"If God wanted to take me home that night, He would have."

"If you don't get more rest He still might," Taylor said. "You men can come visit again tomorrow."

"Bring Topper around to the window so he can see I'm all right when you come back," Vic said. "He frets a lot if we're apart for too long."

"We'll do that," Zee said.

"Out! All of you!" Taylor ordered.

The lamp was turned low, the curtains drawn so the room was dimly lit. Vic lay back on his pillow, made the Sign of the Cross, and began fingering his rosary.

Until I find the right one, settle down and get married, this is the only woman I need in my life. Gracias, Bendita Madre, Nuestra Senora de Guadalupe.

Author's Notes

Much of the historical information in this novel comes from The Texas Historical Commission and Texas State Historical Association, both of which I am crediting here.

Wyatt Earp, Doc Holliday, Bat Masterson, and Big Nose Kate did indeed spend time in Fort Griffin, along with many other notorious figures of the Old West. It was here where Holliday and Kate first met, and established a common law relationship that would end only with his death.

The confrontation between Vic Verdugo, Earp, Holliday, and Masterson in the text is of course fictitious.

I have also taken some literary license with the setting. Some of the buildings and businesses mentioned were not established until a few years after the time this story is set.

About the Author

James J. Griffin is a lifelong New Englander, but has been a student of the Frontier West, in particular the Texas Rangers, from a young age. He has travelled to all fifty states, most extensively in Texas and the Southwest to research the settings for his stories, including many horseback riding trips. Authenticity, within the realm of fiction, is a hallmark of Griffin's work.

Jim is a lifelong horseman, including serving as a volunteer with the Connecticut State Horse Patrol. He has owned four American Paint Horses. Horses are always an integral part of his writing. He is also a five-time finalist for the Western Fictioneers Peacemaker Awards. He is a member of the Western Writers of America and Western Fictioneers.

A graduate of Notre Dame High School in West Haven, CT and Southern Connecticut State University, Jim now makes his home in Keene, New Hampshire.

Center Point Large Print
600 Brooks Road / PO Box 1
Thorndike, ME 04986-0001 USA

(207) 568-3717

US & Canada:
1 800 929-9108
www.centerpointlargeprint.com